"*Kari Lynn's Shattered Dreams* is a heartfelt book about a Christian couple's journey through dreams broken, forgiveness, and God's transforming grace."

— Carol Willits, former director of *CareNet Pregnancy Resource Center*

"*Kari Lynn's Shattered Dreams* sketches a critical yet often hidden struggle in today's society: post abortion syndrome. Delaine Swardstrom gently guides the reader through the physical, emotional, and spiritual struggles of a post abortive couple, leading us through their dark and twisty path of grief."

— Kristin Smith, Executive Director of the *National Memorial for the Unborn*

Kari Lynn's SHATTERED DREAMS

DELAINE SWARDSTROM

KARI LYNN'S SHATTERED DREAMS

ISBN:9781503086401

For more about Delaine Swardstrom visit — www.BooksByDelaine.com
Cover model photography: Delaine Swardstrom
Cover model: Brittany Jones

Printed in the United States of America.

To Brenda.
Thank you for the choice
you made. I love you.

acknowledgements

I began writing this story several years ago. One day my husband, *Jack*, suggested I write a book about abortion. Although I don't think *Kari Lynn's Shattered Dreams* is exactly what he had in mind when he made this suggestion, nonetheless I still give him credit. It set me working on the book again, getting it ready for publication. Jack, I know you put up with a lot while I was working on this book, writing, rewriting, and editing. The house wasn't always as straight as I might have liked, and meals often lacked originality. And I know you didn't like it when I chased you out of my computer room when I was trying to concentrate. But we managed to make it. I hope you like my finished product.

Next I must certainly give credit to my *Heavenly Father*. It was He who put the story in my head. I could never have written this book without Him. Many times I wondered where the story needed to go from here, and viola, an idea came to me. I know it was none of my doing, but His. The forgiveness Kari Lynn and Troy experienced in this story is something we can all experience ourselves. I thank God He is so willing to forgive us the many times we grieve Him. Thank You, Lord, for Your great salvation that is available as a free gift to all who accept it. May this book be an honor to Him and glorify His name.

Of course I must give credit to my friend, *Tamara Clymer*. Thank you for having enough faith in me to offer to help me publish this book, even if it was far from ready for publication when you first saw it. I know you wondered many times if you were biting off more than you could chew, but you still believed in me. Thank you for that confidence.

I definitely cannot forget to mention *Pamela Sonnenmoser*, my writing coach. She has recently gone to be with the Lord but we will never forget her. I'm sure she too wondered if I was worth working with as week by week we went over the chapters of this book. I cannot thank her enough for all the help she gave me, not just for *Kari Lynn's Shattered Dreams*, but for my writing in general. I only wish Pamela was here to see the finished product. I hope she would have been pleased with the result of her work with me.

I also need to thank the *staff at Bethany Christian Services*, as well as *Adoption Minnesota*, for their valuable help with information about adoption. This is an area I'm not familiar with and without their information and advice I'm afraid my writing would not be accurate.

My neighbors, *Derrick and Renee*, helped me with information about Kari Lynn's surgery. Although I'm a registered nurse myself so much has changed since I worked in a hospital I needed their expertise. Thank you for your input.

Thanks also to *Carol* and my sister, *Ethel*, for reading through my manuscript. It always helps to have fresh sets of eyes review what I've written.

There are others, individuals who wish to remain anonymous, who answered my questions to provide accuracy in my writing.

And to *my readers*, thank you for reading this book. I pray it will be an inspiration to you. I would love to hear from my readers and learn what they think of my book. You can e-mail me at booksbydelaine@yahoo.com. Or contact me on Facebook at Books by Delaine.

prologue

A wave of nostalgia came over Kari Lynn Moore as she pushed herself into the tree house nestled in the branches of an old maple. She hadn't visited her childhood retreat in several years, but it was just as she remembered. It was nothing elaborate; just four walls, a floor, and a roof. Windows in two sides let in light and kept out most of the wind and rain. A ladder next to the trunk of the tree allowed entrance through an opening in one corner of the floor.

Her family spent most of their summers at their lakeside cabin on the edge of the National Forest in Northern Minnesota. She remembered the year her dad built the playhouse for her and her brother. The first few years she and Dan enjoyed the hideaway together, playing their make-believe games. Later he decided he was too old for such childish things and found interests elsewhere.

As a young girl she spent countless hours here, often curled up in the corner of a battered, overstuffed chair with a favorite book. It was also a place to hide when she tired of her brother's incessant teasing.

It was a cozy retreat for her as she was growing up, but now she stood on the brink of adulthood. In three weeks she would move into the dorm and start classes at the University of Minnesota.

She crossed the floor and made her way toward the chair in the corner. Ignoring the layer of dust and dry leaves covering the surface, she sank into the sagging, brown tweed cushions.

Life had been good for Kari Lynn. Until now. Her father, an English professor, was tired of the long Minnesota winters. When asked to chair the English department at a small college in California, he jumped at the opportunity. Now they were moving away. They had come to the cabin to enjoy a few days of relaxation, away from the stress of packing for the move.

Why did her parents have to move to Bakersfield just when she was about to begin college? She always counted on them being close by so she could go home on weekends. But that was over now. California was too far from Minneapolis. And since she planned to work part time during the school year, she would consider herself fortunate if she could even visit them at Christmas.

Her mind wandered as she settled in the old chair. Almost with a mind of its own, her hand slid behind the cushions. She was surprised to find a tattered spiral notebook still there. In it were all of her private musings and dreams for the future. A smile came to her lips when she remembered all the plans she made for her life. She would meet a handsome man, get married, and raise a beautiful family. Even that was planned. Two boys and two girls were her idea of the perfect combination.

Alternating between smiles and tears, she leafed through the pages. One page caught her attention and she stopped to read the childish scrawl. The day she wrote it came to mind as if it was this morning. Furious with her older brother's persistent teasing, she lashed out in anger. The result was a heated argument and she felt she hadn't a friend in the world. Her dad came to the tree house and found her crying. He cuddled her on his lap, as he so often did, and told her about the best Friend she could have. One who would never disappoint her the way Dan had. She opened her heart to Jesus that afternoon. A tear slipped down her cheek, but it went unnoticed as she read what she wrote later that day.

> *Today I asked Jesus to be my best Friend, and I know that He is. I'm never going to forget Him. He will be my very best Friend for the rest of my life. I'll forever do exactly what He wants. His book, the Bible, will be my favorite book from now on and I will read it EVERY day. I promise.*

For the most part she'd kept those promises. Not many days went by that she didn't read and study what God had written. And she intended to continue, even now when she was ready to start out on her own.

She allowed a loud sigh to escape when she realized it was time to put away her childish dreams and look ahead to the reality of life as an adult. Growing up wasn't easy. A tear trickled down her cheek when she thought about her parents moving so far away. She would miss them. Her dad most of all since the two of them were exceptionally close.

Her mother's voice floated through the trees interrupting her thoughts.

"Kari Lynn, we're ready to leave. Come on."

"Be right there, Mom."

She hugged her journal to her chest and wiped away another tear.

"Yes, Lord," she whispered, "You were a friend to me ever since that day. I met You up here in this old tree house many times since then, and You always helped me solve the problems of growing up. Help me keep those promises I made that day. I do want to live a life that will please You. Help me keep my eyes on You …"

"Are you up here, Kari Lynn?"

Her father's voice at the base of the ladder interrupted her prayer. She managed to stuff her journal behind the cushions seconds before her dad's head appeared in the opening. As far as she knew no one else was aware the book existed.

Tall, slender, sandy-haired Mr. Moore pulled himself into the room. Everyone said she favored her father in looks with her blond hair and blue eyes. The sight of his tender smile brought more tears. She was going to miss the good times and long talks she shared with this man. Especially as she struggled with the trials of teen age years.

Walking across the room she threw her arms around him.

"What's wrong, Kitten?"

A smile managed to peek through her tears. When was the last time she heard him call her that childhood nickname?

The familiar spicy scent of his after-shave enveloped her as she snuggled her head in his shoulder, settling into the strong arms wrapped around her.

"I'm going to miss you so when you move. Why do you have to go so far away?" She sniffed back more tears. "I wish I didn't have to grow up. Why can't things stay the way they are forever?"

Mr. Moore stroked her hair and pulled her closer.

"I know it's difficult," he whispered, "but it is an inevitable part of life. You'll make it, just like the rest of us have. Keep your eyes on Jesus and everything will be okay. If you forget everything else I taught you, I hope you never forget that one important principle."

"I won't, Daddy. He was my best Friend all these years. I

don't expect to change now."

"That's my girl. Even though your mom and I are far away, remember, He's only a prayer away." He planted a kiss on the top of her head, then took her hand and led her toward the ladder. "Come now, we must be going. Your mother is anxious to leave."

She took one last look around the familiar tree house. Yes, childhood was over and a new life lay ahead of her. But she knew she would never be alone. Her best Friend would always be at her side.

chapter 1

"You're going to be all right now. It's all over."

Troy reached across the console to take Kari Lynn's hand. She snatched it away. He didn't miss the glare she sent his way as she scrunched her shoulder against the passenger door as though intending to put as much distance between them as possible. Her hands were clasped into fists so tight her nails dug into the palms.

He pulled the car up near the entrance of Parkview Apartments and cut the engine.

"Are you ready to go in, or do you want to go get something to eat first?"

Before he could pull the key from the ignition, she threw her door open, almost falling to the ground in her rush to get out. Without a word, she slammed it behind her and marched toward the building, her back straight and arms stiff at her sides. He jumped out and jogged up the walk to catch up with her. She only quickened her step.

Jerking the front door open, she stomped inside. The heavy oak slab slammed in his face as he started to follow, the force pushing him back a step.

Whoa! This is not the Kari Lynn he knew. Her anger was almost palpable. The girl he knew was always patient and kind, not someone easily angered. It was obvious she didn't want him near her. He shook his head, unable to believe what was happening.

After standing outside for several minutes trying to decide if he should follow her, he turned and retraced his steps to the car. Although he hated to leave her alone after what she just went through, he knew she would be okay. What she needed now was rest. He could check on her later.

He started the engine and drove down the street. A few minutes later he pulled up in front of his own building. But even as he walked up the stairs to his apartment, his mind was back with Kari Lynn.

Kari Lynn rubbed her eyes and looked around. Still half asleep, she wondered why she didn't hear the waves lapping on the shore and the buzz of all the people laughing and talking. Not even the sea gulls screamed in the air. Everything was quiet.

Then her gaze came to rest on the blue couch and the desk with her computer, and she realized she was in her apartment. She wasn't at the beach with Troy. That was only a dream.

Her eyes wandered around the room. She loved her apartment with the large windows looking out over the city. The warm, beige walls and tan carpet were comforting. The burgundy recliner she was sitting in was comfortable, her favorite place to rest.

She shook her head to clear the fogginess, wondering how long she'd been asleep. A glance at the cell phone beside her told her it was almost two o'clock. More than two hours went past while she slept. She snuggled deeper into the cushions of the chair. It felt good to relax after the stress of the last several days.

Her gaze wandered to the picture of Troy on the end table. She stared at it for several minutes before forcing her eyes away. It might be best if she put it away. There was no future for them now. At least that's what he told her the night she gave him the news.

Images of this morning began to float through her mind. She couldn't believe what she did.

Forcing herself out of the chair, she made her way across the room. There was no way she could stay here. It would give her too much time to think. She needed to go somewhere, anywhere to get away from everything.

After closing the apartment door behind her, she made her way down the long hallway. She had no idea where she was going, but it didn't matter.

When she reached the elevator and put out her hand to push the call button, she caught a glimpse of her reflection in the shiny doors. A lock of thick, blond hair hung over her eyes. She shoved it aside and gasped. Makeup was smeared all over her face!

I can't let anyone see me like this.

Although she scrubbed at it with her fingers, that only made it worse. With a sigh she shrugged her shoulders and pushed the button again. She shifted from one foot to the other as she waited for the elevator to come. What took it so long? Although she loved her apartment on the twenty-ninth floor where she could look out over the city, she hated this wait for the elevator.

The door finally opened and she stepped inside, relieved to find she was alone. At least she wouldn't have to carry on small talk with anyone. Her thoughts began to drift to the day she met Troy. A half-hearted smile flitted across her face as she recalled her first glimpse of the tall, handsome man standing in the church doorway. He looked lost as he glanced around, running his fingers through his reddish-blond hair.

She still couldn't believe he was with the group of singles who went out for lunch after church that day. Even now, two years later, her pulse quickened when she remembered those mischievous green eyes that looked into hers when he slipped into the chair next to her. His easy going, fun loving personality captivated her at once.

It took effort, but she managed to push both the smile and the memories aside. He'd changed. The man she knew would never do this to her. He loved life. Why the sudden change of heart? Her lips tightened into a thin line. She could never forgive him. Not after what he forced her to do. It would be best if she forgot Troy Hoffman, forget she ever loved him.

Anger overwhelmed her. At Troy, at herself, and right now she wasn't too fond of God either.

"Where were You, God? Why did You let this happen?" she seethed as she mentally shook a fist toward heaven. "Why didn't you stop us? You would have if You cared."

The elevator reached the lobby and she stumbled a bit, but barely noticed it as she plodded toward the front door. She stepped outside into a cold, October wind. It bit into her tear dampened cheeks as an icy rain, typical of Minnesota autumn, sent shivers spiraling through her body.

I should go get a jacket.

But she ignored the thought and hurried across the parking lot. Seconds later her tan chinos and maroon college sweatshirt were soaked. Oblivious to her surroundings she hunched her shoulders into the wind and forced her feet down the sidewalk. She had no idea where they were taking her, but it didn't matter. Life as she knew it was now over.

Her feet slipped when they hit the wet grass of a nearby park. The world around her began to fade and her stomach churned. She grabbed the arm of a bench and collapsed in the corner seconds before falling. Drawing her feet up unto the seat, she hugged her knees close to her chest. Thoughts of Troy skittered through her mind. If only he was with her. But she knew he would never be there for her again.

An uncontrollable shiver spiraled through her body. Wet hair plastered the sides of her face and her clothes clung to her. Miserable and alone, she wished she could just fade into oblivion. It would be a so much easier to drift into the dark chasm of unconsciousness than have to remember.

Troy shook his head. He still couldn't believe Kari Lynn shut the door in his face. That wasn't like her. But he might as well face the fact she wanted nothing to do with him anymore. At least that's what her actions seemed to tell him.

He slammed the apartment door behind him and crossed the floor, slumping into his brown leather recliner. His gaze roamed around the room, the place he felt so at home. Its masculine décor of browns and tans was perfect for him. It wasn't large, but he didn't need a lot of room for just himself. When he closed his eyes he could almost see Kari Lynn sitting with him on the tweed couch as they held hands, watching their favorite movie. Some evenings they just talked, sharing their deepest thoughts. A glance at the sliding glass door across the room brought back memories of the two of them relaxing in his canvass deck chairs on the balcony, enjoying a cool drink on a warm summer night.

The two of them had a great relationship from day one. He couldn't suppress a smile as he recalled the day he met her. It was his first Sunday after his move to Minneapolis, his first time to attend Calvary Baptist Church.

The moment he stepped inside the door he saw her. She was talking and laughing with some of her friends. Everyone else milling around the foyer became a blur. He couldn't take his eyes off her. The light blue dress she wore, the same color as her eyes, accented her slim figure. Long, blond hair framed a beautiful face. And she was tall, her head a good two or three inches above her friends.

Someone spoke to him and he jumped, pulling himself back to his surroundings. A young man shook his hand and introduced himself, then invited him to join him in one of the Sunday school classes.

The moment he walked in the door he saw her, and his heart skipped a beat. He was sure his face must have lit up when he heard the musical sound of her laughter as she shared something with one of her friends. Yes, he was going to like it here.

After church someone invited him to join several of them for lunch. He jumped at the chance. Maybe she would be there.

The minute he walked in the door of the restaurant he saw her. And the chair next to her was empty! Dashing across the room he couldn't believe his luck as he claimed the spot before anyone else could.

A streak of lightening flashed across the sky and the clap of thunder following it rattled the windows, bringing him back to the present. The good memories were suddenly pushed aside by bad ones. His mind began to replay the events of the past few weeks. If only those days were nothing more than a nightmare, but he knew they weren't.

As he wandered around his apartment he stopped every few minutes to look out the window, hardly aware of the heavy rain streaming down the other side of the pane. With a heavy sigh he dropped back into his recliner. It was hard to believe he pushed the woman he loved into a physical relationship. He knew it was wrong. And if that wasn't bad enough, he was still in shock by her announcement two nights ago. Those few minutes began to play across his mind like a movie on a screen.

"Troy," Kari Lynn said, her lips quivering as she pushed aside a tear trickling down her cheek. "I...I'm pregnant."

Certain his mouth was hanging open he could only stare at her.

"You're what? How can you be?"

"Well what did you expect after what we were doing? Things like this happen, you know."

He forced his gaping mouth shut.

"It must be a mistake."

"I thought so too at first. But I took one of those tests. I'm certain now."

"So what are you going to do?" He frowned at her as he scratched his head.

She shrugged. "What can I do? Maybe you should have thought of that a couple of months ago when you insisted I sleep with you."

The comment caught him off guard. He glared at her.

"We're going to be parents, Troy, whether we like or not."

"There's no way you can have this baby. What will all our friends think?"

"What choice do we have? I'm pregnant, and that means I'm going to have a baby."

After running his fingers through his hair several times

he began to pace the floor. Four trips across his living room later he turned to face her.

"Have an abortion."

Her mouth dropped open.

"What? There's no way I can do that."

"You're going to have to. It's the only way we'll be able to face everyone."

"No! It's wrong. I won't do it."

"It's for your own good."

Several more paces across the room later, he added, "It isn't easy to raise a child alone, you know."

"What do you mean? I thought we were getting married. We have talked about it."

"I never had any intention of marrying you," he muttered and turned away.

The shocked expression on her face when he looked at her again nearly stopped him in his tracks. Tears ran down her face, but she didn't seem to notice.

"But I...I thought...you said..."

He rubbed his forehead and paced some more before turning to her again.

"Well you thought wrong. I don't love you. I never have. Have the abortion and you'll never have to see me again."

Troy slammed his fist on the arm of the recliner. He called himself a Christian. What was he thinking? Guilt weighed him down like an anchor.

Sliding from the chair to his knees, he cried out, "God, I blew it. Not only did I sin, but I pulled Kari Lynn down with me. Please don't let her suffer because of me. And Lord, don't let me lose her. Even though it seemed she couldn't stand the sight of me this morning, I still need to be with her. We're in this together."

How he loved that girl. More than life itself. But now it looked as though everything was over.

A thought came to him and he jumped to his feet. Maybe all was not lost after all. Just because she let the door slam in his face didn't mean everything was over between them. Certainly she would come to her senses and realize they needed each other.

His mind made up, he grabbed his coat and car keys. He had to see her and make things right.

The drive to her apartment didn't take long, despite the rain now coming down in torrents. But the closer he got, the more uneasy he became. He did tell her he wouldn't see her again if she would have the abortion, but he hadn't meant it. Even if she didn't want to see him, he had to at least make an effort to settle things between them. It couldn't end like this.

He pulled up in front of her apartment building, jumped out, and dashed through the pouring rain and in the front door. With his finger suspended over the elevator button, his mind whirled.

Maybe this isn't the best thing to do right now. She might be sleeping. Rest would be good for her. It might be best to come back a little later.

The door opened as he was still contemplating the best course of action. He stepped inside before he lost his nerve. All the way up to the twenty-ninth floor he muttered words of encouragement to himself in an attempt to bolster his courage. Something he sorely lacked at the moment.

When the elevator stopped and he stepped off he bumped into a woman with an armful of bags.

"Sorry," he mumbled.

Pulling in a deep breath, he forced his feet down the hallway to Kari Lynn's apartment.

There was no sound of life when he arrived — no radio or TV. But she had to be there. Surely she wouldn't go anywhere this soon. Especially not in this weather.

Seconds ticked by before he mustered the courage to lift his hand and knock. There was no answer. He rapped again, a little harder this time.

"It's me, Troy. Please open up."

There was still no answer when he knocked again.

Defeated, he made his way back down to the lobby. He knew he promised her she wouldn't have to see him again. Obviously, she took him at his word.

I never even had a chance to tell her I was sorry.

The heavy, gray sky echoed his mood as he started the car and slowly made his way out of the parking lot. If she wasn't going to talk to him there nothing else he could do but pray and wait.

When he neared a small park he caught sight of someone huddled on one of the benches. He couldn't believe anyone would be out here in this miserable weather.

As he turned the corner he slowed down, craning his neck for a better look.

"Kari Lynn!"

Skidding the car to a stop, he jumped out and sprinted toward the bench, slipping on the rain-soaked grass. Just as he reached her, she slumped forward. He was barely able to catch her before she could tumble to the ground.

chapter 2

Troy eased the crumpled body back onto the bench. He yanked off his jacket, wrapped it around her, and pulled her to him.

Fear gripped him as she lay limp in his arms.

"Oh, God, don't let her be..."

A trembling finger at the side of her neck told him there was a pulse. It wasn't strong, but at least she was alive.

Shaking her gently, he shouted, "Kari Lynn, speak to me!"

No response.

"Oh God, please don't let anything happen to her."

He knew he had to do something, but what?

Frantically he waved an arm toward the street.

"Help! Somebody help me!"

But the cars continued on their way. They didn't even slow down to see what was wrong.

Not knowing what else to do, he grabbed his cell phone off his belt. Somehow his trembling fingers managed to dial the number.

"Nine-one-one, what's your emergency?"

"I need an ambulance! Now!"

After shouting directions to the operator, he gathered Kari

Lynn into his arms and raced across the park toward his car. Twice he slipped and almost dropped her. But he raced on, his shoes sloshing through puddles with each step.

In his rush his feet slid off the wet curb when he reached to open the rear door and her head barely missed hitting the top of the vehicle. He laid her gently on the back seat. She didn't move.

"Oh God," he prayed as he leaned his head against the top of the car. "Let her be all right."

The wail of sirens echoed through the air. Flashes of red and blue lights reflected on the rain-soaked street. He dashed into the road and waved his arms to attract their attention.

"Thank you, Lord," he breathed as an ambulance pulled up behind his car.

"Did you call 9-1-1?" a paramedic asked.

"Yes, I did."

"What's the problem?"

Troy motioned toward his open car door.

"I don't know what's wrong. I saw her sitting here and she just collapsed in my arms. Please, help her."

His heart pounded in his chest as he watched the EMT go through a preliminary exam. Then they lifted her out of the car, laid her on the stretcher, and loaded her in the ambulance. One of them started an IV while the other hooked her to a monitor.

He started to climb in after them.

"Are you her husband?"

"No."

"I'm sorry sir, you'll have to follow us in your car."

"No. I can't let her out of my sight."

The door slammed and the wail of the siren told him otherwise.

As the ambulance started to pull away he shook his head to

collect his thoughts. Coming to his senses, he jerked his driver's door open and jumped into the seat, shoved the shift lever into drive and spun away from the curb. A chill slithered up his spine from his wet clothes, but he paid no attention. He tailed the ambulance to the hospital, oblivious to the posted speed limit.

"It's all my fault. Please, God, let her be all right."

Emergency room workers ran to meet the ambulance as soon as it pulled up to the door. Troy screeched to a stop in the closest parking spot and jumped out. The paramedics unloaded the gurney and he watched them wheel Kari Lynn through the heavy glass doors.

When he started to follow, a nurse in blue scrubs stepped in front of him.

"Are you her husband?"

"No. I'm...I'm her friend. I found her in the park and called the ambulance."

She put a hand on his arm and eased him toward to the check-in counter.

"You can't go in the treatment area if you aren't family. But you can help her by giving me some information. Do you know her name?"

"Kari Lynn Moore."

"Do you know what happened?"

First the ambulance people and now this woman. He was tired of answering questions.

"No, I don't." His mind was distracted as he kept his gaze on the doors. "I was driving past the park when I saw her crumpled on a bench. By the time I got to her she was unconscious."

They needed more information than that he was sure, but he didn't know what else to tell them. She seemed fine when he left this morning. At least physically. But he had no idea what happened after that.

I should have stayed with her. I could have kept something like this from happening.

He started toward the door again. The nurse grabbed his arm.

"Sir, you can't go in there. Why don't you have a seat in the waiting room?" Her face told him she meant business.

After one more glance at those formidable doors, he forced his feet across the floor. Gray upholstered chairs were clustered in groups around the room. A few people were seated here and there, some crying, others talking among themselves. Oblivious to anyone else, he slumped into one of the chairs, releasing a sigh from deep within. Something must have happened with the abortion. But she seemed okay when he left her at the apartment building.

He shook his head in frustration.

I should have insisted she let me stay with her, whether she wanted me to or not.

"Dear God, be with the doctors and nurses," he whispered. "I don't know what she was doing out there in that cold rain, but thank You for bringing me along just when You did."

His gaze kept straying toward the treatment area. If only someone would bring him some news. When it didn't happen he forced himself to stay seated. The doctors and nurses were doing the best they could. There was no need for him to be in the way, no matter how much he wanted to be there. He knew worrying didn't help, but he couldn't seem to stop. Although he tried to leave Kari Lynn in God's hands, it was difficult.

What if I never see her again? What if she...?

The thought that he might lose her nearly crushed him. He was the one who pushed her to have the abortion and he couldn't blame her if she hated him. But now if she didn't survive, that would be his fault too.

Tears dripped between his fingers as he buried his face in his hands.

"Please let Kari Lynn be okay, God. Give us one more chance. Please. Give me an opportunity to make everything up to her."

Unable to sit still any longer, he wandered into the hallway. A sign pointing to the hospital chapel caught his eye and he made his way in that direction.

❁❁❁

Kari Lynn tried to force her eyes open against the assault of the bright lights above her. A firm grip restrained her when she tried to raise her hand to shield her eyes.

"You need to lie still."

She tried to focus, but everything was fuzzy.

"Wh...where am I?"

"You're in the emergency room at St. Luke's."

The bright lights made her squint as she attempted to look around. Nothing was familiar. Someone in blue scrubs fussed over her, checking her blood pressure and who knew what else. A faint aroma of antiseptic permeated the air. Through the narrow space where the curtain was pushed aside she could make out people in scrubs rushing around. Monitors beeped close by. She must be in the hospital, but how did she get here?

Shaking her head she attempted to clear her mind. The last thing she remembered was sitting on a park bench in the rain, half frozen. After that…

"Wh…what am I doing in…in an emergency room? I…I don't remember coming…"

"Someone brought you," the person beside her explained. "Do you remember what happened?"

"I don… don't know."

A bag of dark red fluid hanging above her caught her attention. She let her eyes follow the tubing down to her arm. Another bag of clear liquid dripped into her other hand.

"Wh… what's this?" Frantic, her eyes searched the faces around her. "What happened to me?"

"We hoped you could tell us. We ran some tests and your hemoglobin is very low. We're running more now to find out why."

She hid her face in her hands. Everything was so confusing.

"Is there a chance you might be pregnant?"

The nurse's question broke through the fog. All the events of the last few days came flooding back.

When she closed her eyes in an attempt to block out the memories, parades of tiny babies began to march behind her closed lids. They cried and pointed accusing fingers at her.

Her eyes flew open.

"Get them out of here!" she screamed as she scrambled to get off the bed. "Make them stop! I can't stand it!"

Firm, but kind hands held her down.

"Just lie still. You're safe here. No one can hurt you here."

The kind voice belonged to the young woman in blue scrubs standing beside her bed. Kari Lynn reached out to her.

"Please, help me," she whispered.

"Tell me what has you so frightened."

The nurse's calm voice began to dispel some of her fear and her taut muscles started to relax.

"We're here to help you, but you have to tell us what has you so afraid. Did someone try to hurt you?"

"Yes!" she shouted, then hesitated a moment. "No," she said

in a hoarse whisper. "No one hurt me. I guess I hurt myself."

"You hurt yourself? What did you do?"

Hot tears ran from the corners of her eyes and slid into her ears before she could brush them away. She closed her eyes, hoping when she opened them again it was just a dream. But when she peeked between her lids again nothing had changed, except that now a strange, gray haired man stood beside her bed.

"I… I had an abortion this morning," she whispered. "I was supposed to stay at home and rest, but instead I went for a walk."

"We need to get her to surgery," the man shouted as he rushed out into the hall. "Now!"

Feet scurried around the room while muffled voices added to her confusion.

A nurse appeared at her bedside.

"Can you sign this consent form? We need your permission to do surgery. Do you have any family here? A husband or anyone who should know?"

"No, there's no one."

"Maybe the man who brought you," the nurse suggested.

"The man who brought me?" She looked from one person to another. "Who brought me? I wasn't with anyone."

She cocked her head to the side and tried to think.

"I do kind of remember someone calling my name, but I don't know who it was."

It certainly wasn't Troy. He left as soon as he brought her home from the clinic. It must be someone else.

Before she could consider it further, a pen was pushed into her hand. Tears blurred the page as she signed her name on what she hoped was the right line. She didn't even know what she was signing.

Confused and angry, she looked from one face to another.

"Why am I going to surgery? Someone tell me what's going on."

A man laid a hand on her arm.

"I'm Dr. Young. Someone found you collapsed on a park bench and realized you were in trouble. He called 9-1-1 and the ambulance brought you here. You weren't conscious when you first arrived and we didn't know what was wrong. We couldn't get much information from the man who brought you. He said he didn't know what happened, so we had no idea how to help.

"Now that we know about the abortion it makes sense. You were probably injured during the procedure. We're taking you to surgery to see what kind of damage was done. You may be hemorrhaging internally. If that's the case, we may have to remove your uterus."

The words hit her with the force of an exploding time bomb.

"Wait! You can't do that. I want to have children some day! There must be some mistake."

The room began to spin and the bitter taste of bile rose in the back of her throat. Her whole body trembled. She tried to force herself to a sitting position, but hands eased her back down.

"We won't do anything more than absolutely necessary," the doctor assured her, "but you do need to know it is a possibility. If there's too much damage we won't have a choice. It may be the only way to save your life."

She couldn't listen anymore.

I don't want to live if I can never have children. That's all I ever wanted. My life will be ruined.

Another blue-clad nurse appeared at the bedside with a syringe in her hand.

"I'm going to give you a sedative to get you ready for surgery."

She pushed the needle into the IV tubing and looked at Kari Lynn before pushing the plunger.

"Are you sure there's no one we should notify? A family member or a friend?"

Maybe Troy should know. But no, he told her she would never have to see him again if she had the abortion. He wouldn't care what happened to her. And she definitely didn't want her parents to know. They would be devastated.

"No, there's no one," she sighed.

The nurse injected the sedative and she felt herself slowly slip into unconsciousness. Perhaps it would be for good this time.

Troy stepped into the small hospital chapel. As his eyes adjusted to the dim light they were immediately drawn to a backlit cross on the front wall. He slowly made his way down the short aisle between rows of pews and dropped to his knees.

"Father, I know I've messed up, but I also know You are willing to forgive me. For everything." Tears streamed down his face but he ignored them. "Thank You that You are willing to forgive even our most heinous sins."

Time stood still as he talked to his Heavenly Father, something he had neglected the last few months. He bared his soul with everything on his heart: the baby, the abortion, his relationship with Kari Lynn, and his concern for her.

"Be with her, Father. I don't know what's wrong, but You do. Please, keep her safe."

His head hurt and his knees ached from being on them so long, but he felt a sense of relief. Jesus now carried the burden.

"Thank You for loving me, even when I knowingly mess up. Help me keep my eyes on You. I don't ever want to stray so far again."

As he got to his feet and turned to leave he noticed a door at the back of the room with a sign, Chaplain's Office. Funny he hadn't noticed it before. Maybe someone there could help him make sense of all of this.

He hesitated outside the partially closed door before lifting his hand to knock.

"Come in," a voice called.

Troy pushed the door open. A middle-aged man in wire-rim glasses sat behind a desk. A young woman was in a nearby chair.

"Oh, I...I'm sorry." He backed away. "I...I didn't mean to interrupt. I…I can wait."

"Come on in," The woman stood and extended her hand. "You're not interrupting. I work in the chaplain's office. I'm Laura Brownlee, one of the lay workers." She nodded toward the man behind the desk. "And this is Chaplin Barnes."

"Troy Hoffman," he said as he shook their hands. He hesitated, unsure what he should say.

"I… I wondered if I could talk to someone," he began.

The chaplain leaned forward.

"That's what we're here for." He motioned toward a chair at the corner of the desk. "Have a seat and let's see how we can help you. Do you have someone in the hospital?

"Yes. In the emergency room. I… the ambulance just brought her in."

Slowly he began to tell his story. As it unfolded, he found himself sharing what transpired in his life with Kari Lynn over the last few months.

"The thing is, we both believe God's Word and try to live for Him." He ran his fingers through his hair. "How did we let ourselves get caught up in all of this?"

Chaplain Barnes leaned his elbows on the desk, his hands

tented together in front of him. "It's not hard to understand. As Christians we're tempted just the same as everyone else."

"Yes, I know. But I love that girl. How could I do this to someone I love?"

The chaplain rested a hand on his arm.

"I'm afraid I can't answer that question for you, son. But you're not the first Christian this happened to, and sorry to say you won't be the last, I'm sure."

Troy nodded and closed his eyes. He wasn't sure what else to say. "I know God has forgiven me. But Kari Lynn doesn't want to see me. She made that very clear this morning. I want to help her, but how can I when she won't talk to me?"

Laura leaned forward in her chair.

"Maybe I can help. That's why I'm here — to help women like her. Do you know if she was admitted?"

He shook his head.

"I don't know what happened. They wouldn't let me see her. But I doubt she would be released. She was in pretty bad shape."

Laura picked up the phone and dialed a number. A few minutes later she had the answer. "They took her to surgery an hour ago," she said as she put the instrument back.

"Surgery!" His mouth dropped open as he stared at her. "What kind of surgery?"

"I don't know. They can't give me much information. She'll be in recovery soon, though. If you like, I can take you to the waiting room. You could talk to the doctor when he's finished in surgery. Maybe he will give you more information. Then when she's moved to a room on the surgical floor you can see her."

He rubbed his chin.

"I don't know if it would be a good idea for me to see her. Not right now, anyway." He realized he sounded uncaring, so added,

"I'm afraid we're not on the best of terms at the moment."

His arms ached to hold her, but it might be best if he went on home. At least for now. When he glanced down he noticed how damp and wrinkled his clothes were.

"Anyway, I think I need to get into something different. I'm pretty much of a mess right now. Could you look in on her? I'm sure she will need someone. I just don't think I'm that person right now. This morning she seemed pretty upset with me, and I doubt her mood has changed. I don't want to upset her any more than she probably is already. I'll go home and change, then come back and see how she is."

When he stepped out of the chaplain's office he couldn't squelch a feeling of guilt for skipping out on Kari Lynn. But he knew she would sleep off the anesthesia and probably wouldn't even know he was there. It had helped to talk to the chaplain. It did help relieve some of his distress.

A scratchy, day old stubble of beard scraped across his hand when he rubbed it over his face. He needed to get cleaned up.

As he drove away from the hospital the events of the past few days weighed heavy on his mind. The hurt look on Kari Lynn's face when she finally consented to go along with his plan still haunted him. And her expression of guilt and defeat when she walked out after the abortion — that was going to plague him the rest of his life.

When he got home he headed straight for the shower. As the steaming water flowed over his head and down his back he tried to think how he should approach her. She wouldn't be very receptive he was sure. But then he couldn't blame her.

The clock on the bedside stand when he came out of the shower said it was almost three in the morning. Not a good time to go see anyone in the hospital. In fact they probably wouldn't even let him in the building.

Although the bed looked tempting, he was sure he wouldn't sleep even if he lay down. But maybe it wouldn't hurt for a couple of hours. It was a long, trying day. Besides, the rest might help clear his head.

Before laying his head on the pillow he whispered one last prayer. "Lord, I know You have forgiven me. But I still need to make things right with Kari Lynn. Please give me the opportunity, and let her be open to listening."

chapter 3

Troy woke with a jolt. What was that awful noise?

In his sleep numb condition he finally realized it was the alarm. His hand connected with the clock radio sending it crashing to the floor. Frustrated, he kicked off the covers and grabbed the blaring thing. Two tries later there was silence.

Exhausted, he stretched his arms over his head and drew in a deep breath. He twisted his shoulders trying to work out the kinks as the sleepy fog began to release its hold on his brain.

Then it dawned on him. Today was Saturday.

"What am I doing getting up so early?"

Stifling a yawn, he started to lie back down. Before his head even hit the pillow it came to him.

"I can't go back to bed. I need to get to the hospital."

The few short hours of sleep he managed to get were not near enough. But there wasn't time to stay in bed this morning, as enticing as it was.

He headed to the bathroom for another quick shower. The hot, stinging water washed over his back and shoulders, rinsing away the fuzziness of sleep and the tension of the last few days.

"Oh, no, not again," he groaned as his razor died just as he was ready to make a last swipe across his chin.

He threw the appliance on the countertop and brought his head closer to the mirror for a better look.

"That will have to do. No one will notice those few stray whiskers anyway."

Not sure how long Kari Lynn would be in the hospital he knew he needed to get there before she was released. It might be his only real chance to talk to her. Even if she didn't want to see him she couldn't very well keep him out of her room without making a scene.

After quickly dressing he picked up a jacket, locked his apartment, and jogged to his car.

When he arrived at the hospital he stopped at the information desk to find out her room number. As he made his way up to the third floor he wondered what he would find. Would she even talk to him?

Stepping off the elevator he looked up and down the hall. An arrow pointed the way to room 335.

He stopped.

Maybe this isn't such a good idea. What if I make things worse by coming?

But he shook off the fear and forced his feet down the corridor.

Before reaching for the knob he stopped in front of her door and whispered a silent prayer. When he raised his head, a man dressed in green scrubs was coming down the hall and turned toward the room.

"Are you Kari Lynn Moore's doctor?"

"Yes, I'm Dr. Gordon."

"Troy Hoffman" he said as he grabbed the doctor's hand in a firm shake. "How is she? Is everything all right?"

"Are you her husband?"

"No, we aren't married. At least not yet. I...the baby...the..." he stuttered, not sure just what to say. "Can you tell me what happened? What's going on?"

"I'm sorry, but if you aren't her husband I can't tell you anything unless she gives me permission." He nodded toward the room. "I'm on my way to see her now. If you would like I can ask if she'll let me share the results of the surgery with you."

"Yes, please do." Troy took a deep breath. "Can...can I see her?"

"Let me see if she feels up to it. If she agrees, you may visit for a little while."

He nodded, and watched as the doctor stepped into the room. It was all he could do to stay behind.

Kari Lynn struggled to open her eyes.

"Where am I?"

Nothing looked familiar. The last thing she remembered was a nurse smiling down at her in the emergency room and beeping monitors in the background. Now, everything was quiet. Too quiet. She gazed out the window. It looked like the sun was just coming up. She must have been asleep for a long time.

A hand touched her arm. She looked up and saw an unfamiliar man beside her bed.

"Hi, Kari Lynn. I'm Dr. Gordon. How are you this morning?"

"Okay… I think. Wh… what happened?" She searched the man's face for answers.

"You're in the hospital. You came to this room from surgery and the recovery room a few hours ago. You'll be all right now, you just need to rest."

"Surg… surgery?" She felt around on her body for bandages or other evidence of an operation but found nothing. "Wh... what did they do? Why did I have surgery?"

"You don't remember going to the operating room?"

She tried to fight through the haze in her brain. A few things came to mind, but they were fuzzy.

"I... I think I remember someone say something about going to surgery. What did they do?"

Then it came to her. She gasped and clamped her hand over her mouth.

"Wait! I think they told me... Did they... did they have to...?"

"We weren't able to repair the damage. You will never be able to have children. I'm sorry."

"What? No! That can't be happening. I want to have a family someday."

She stared at the doctor hoping he was kidding and that this was all nothing but a horrible joke.

But the expression on his face told her otherwise.

"I'm sorry. We tried everything, but there was just no way."

It was impossible to even try to stop the tears that filled her eyes. That was it. Her dreams of a beautiful family were over. There would be no children. No pitter-patter of little feet running to greet her. She would never watch a daughter get married, or hold a brand new grandchild in her arms.

The doctor's voice broke through the pain. "There's a man by the name of Troy out in the hall asking for you."

"Troy's here?"

"Yes. He's quite worried about you. He wants to know what happened. Do I have your permission to talk to him about it?"

"I suppose so. He probably should know."

"He's also anxious to see you. Do you mind if he comes in for a few minutes?"

What could he possibly want? She didn't know what to think. He walked out on her when she needed him most, so what was he doing here now? After all, he was the reason she went through with the abortion. She wasn't sure if she wanted to see him.

She released a frustrated sigh.

"Yes, I guess you can tell him to come in," she whispered.

The doctor turned to leave, his hand resting on the door knob.

"I'll look in on you again when you're a little more awake. Just try to get some rest now."

He turned and stepped into the hall, the door closing softly behind him. A sob escaped her throat. This couldn't be happening. It had to be a bad dream.

❖❖❖

Troy was waiting in the hall just across from the door when the doctor stepped out of the room. In two steps he closed the gap between them.

"How is she?" he asked. "May I see her?"

The doctor nodded.

"For a little while. She's still pretty groggy from the anesthetic so I wouldn't stay long." He turned to leave. "I'll be at the nurse's station for a while if you want to talk to me."

"Thanks, I'll do that."

He hesitated a moment, then quietly pushed the door open and stepped inside. His first glimpse of her made him stop. She lay so still, her long, blond hair splayed across the pillow. Her face looked so pale.

He tiptoed to the side of her bed.

"Kari Lynn?" he whispered as he bent and kissed her cheek.

She opened her eyes and gave him a weak smile.

"Hello, Troy."

"How are you?

"I've been better."

Her eyes focused on him a moment.

"Why are you here?" Her voice was little more than a whisper. "I… I thought you didn't want anything to do with me."

"I want to be here. I love you. More than anything in the world."

Her eyes closed as though she didn't have the energy to hold them open.

"Then why did you tell me you would get out of my life if I'd… if I had the abortion?" she mumbled.

Her voice was so soft he had to come closer to hear her. He took her limp hand in his.

"I'm so sorry. I don't know why I told you that. I guess I was scared and didn't know what to do. But I do love you. I have since the first day we met."

He bent down and pressed a kiss to her forehead.

"Just get well. Despite everything that happened, I love you just as much as ever. Nothing has changed. You rest now, and I'll come back to see you again later."

A tear slipped down her cheek and she slowly swiped it away. She turned her head toward him.

"No, Troy. Everything has changed. I… I'll never be able to have a family."

He stared at her, unable to comprehend what she said. In fact her voice was so soft he wasn't sure he heard her correctly.

"I… I don't understand..."

"Something went wrong during the abortion." Her eyes fluttered closed. "There was too much damage, so they had to remove..." She bit back a sob. "I can never have children."

"You mean..."

It felt as if someone punched him in the stomach and knocked the wind out of him.

Oh, God, what did I do to her?

"I just want to be alone now. Please leave."

"But... but we're in this together..."

"No. It's best if we just say goodbye. It's over."

"You mean..." He couldn't believe what he was hearing.

"Just leave, please. I want to be alone."

His feet felt nailed to the floor and he couldn't move.

"Please go." She turned her head toward the wall and pulled the covers up to her chin. Her silence told him it was time to leave.

He didn't know what to do. It didn't seem right to leave her here alone. She needed him to be here to comfort her, to help her through this difficult situation. But it didn't appear she wanted him.

Slowly he turned and made his way toward the door. His head told him he should give her some space. His heart screamed to go back and wrap his arms around her, proclaim his love to her.

His head won.

Looking back one last time he whispered, "I love you."

Then he stepped into the hall and quietly closed the door. It was the most difficult thing he ever did.

Kari Lynn listened to Troy's footsteps as he made his way down the hall.

It's over.

She'd lost Troy and the chance to ever have children. Just because of one mistake. Now all her dreams were shattered. As far as she was concerned her life was over.

Tears streamed from her eyes and ran into her ears.

"I was going to have a baby," she whispered into the pillow. "If I hadn't listened to him I would still be pregnant and I could even have more children."

Why did she ever agree to the abortion? She should have just walked away. She could have had the baby and raised it on her own, without him. Now, it was too late. Life was no longer worth living. Why didn't they just let her die instead of trying to save her life?

"Why, God?" she asked as she pounded her fist on the mattress. "Why did You let this happen?"

Half-expecting an answer she looked up at the ceiling. But all was quiet. She was all alone. Troy was gone, and now it looked as though God abandoned her as well.

Anger simmered deep within. It was all his fault. If she hadn't listened to him she wouldn't be here now. He was the one pressuring her to sleep with him. And he was the one who insisted she have the abortion.

"You've ruined everything, Troy," she muttered angrily into her pillow. "Everything."

Dr. Gordon put his hand on Troy's shoulder and led him toward a small lounge. He sat in one of the chairs and nodded at the one across from him.

"Is…is she going to be all right?" Troy asked as he lowered himself to the edge of the seat.

"You are aware we took her to surgery last night."

He nodded.

"And the outcome?"

"Yes, she told me. Is she going to be okay?"

"She will never be able to have children. There was too much damage from the abortion. Since she was bleeding internally we had to do the hysterectomy to save her life. I'm sorry."

The bitter taste of bile rose in the back of his throat.

"Will...will she be all right? She's not going to..."

"Yes, she'll be fine. I'm sure it's a shock to her right now. In fact, I don't know if she is fully aware of what happened yet. She's still under the influence of the anesthetic."

The doctor glanced at him.

"It might be good to have someone with her when she is fully awake and able to understand what happened." He got to his feet. "I'm sorry. There was nothing else we could do. I wish it could have turned out different." He turned to make his way down the hall. "I'll keep you posted on her progress."

Troy watched the doctor walk away. Guilt grabbed his heart.

Kari Lynn, I am so sorry.

A hand touched his shoulder and he looked up, surprised to see Laura Brownlee standing beside him.

"Have you seen Kari Lynn this morning?" she asked.

With his mind still consumed with the doctor's words, he merely nodded. After all, what could he say?

She sat down next to him.

"How is she?"

He shook his head, unable to believe the last few minutes.

"She... she'll never be able to have children."

"Oh, no," Laura whispered. "I'm so sorry."

"And it's all because of me."

He dropped his head into his hands.

"Have you seen her?" he asked without looking up.

"I stopped in a little bit ago. I plan to stay with her most of the day."

"Has she talked to you?"

"No. She wasn't awake enough to say much of anything. I'm not sure she even knew I was in the room."

"I just came from there, and she told me to leave. She said it's over between us."

He looked up.

"How can it be? I love that girl. I have to be with her. I'm part of all of this too."

"I know." Laura took a deep breath. "But it might be a good idea to give her some space. For now, anyway."

She laid her hand on his arm.

"Let me talk to her, help her through the initial shock. You say she doesn't want to see you now, but maybe she will feel different later. Remember, if you go in there right now when she doesn't want you there, you could push her further away."

"I didn't think of that, but I suppose you're right." He pulled in a lung full of air, hoping he sounded more convinced than he felt.

"It's just that I feel so responsible for everything. I love her so much, and I want to be there with her."

"I know how you feel. But sometimes we do more damage by doing what we *think* is right. Pray about it. God will show you what to do. I'll be praying too."

She got to her feet.

"I should get back to her. I don't think she should be alone until she comes to grips with what's happened."

"Will you let me know how she's doing?" He pulled a business card out of his wallet and jotted his cell number on the back. "Call me any time, please. If you think she would be at all interested in seeing me, don't hesitate to call."

"I'll do that." She tucked the card in her pocket.

He watched the woman walk down the hall and then turned to go. Nurses and doctors moved up and down the hall but he didn't notice. He could hardly lift his feet as he made his way toward the elevator. It seemed he had walked miles by the time he arrived.

Kari Lynn pulled in a deep breath and tried to pry her eyes open. With a sense of someone else in the room, she turned her head to see who it was. Hopefully not Troy. She wasn't ready to face him again.

A short, brown haired woman, someone she didn't remember ever seeing before, sat in a chair by the window, her head bowed in an attitude of prayer. She looked to be about her own age.

The woman lifted her head, as though aware Kari Lynn was staring at her. She got to her feet, a friendly smile spreading over her face.

"Do you feel better after your nap?"

What is this stranger doing here? Who is she and what does she want?

She pulled the covers up higher under her chin and closed her eyes. Maybe if she pretended to be asleep the woman would go away.

"I'm Laura Brownlee from the chaplain's office." The soft voice gave a sense of compassion. "I was here earlier, but you were asleep. I thought I'd stop back and see if you'd like someone to talk to."

She moved her chair closer to the bed and settled into it.

Just what I need, some nosy person looking for juicy gossip to spread around.

"Do you have someone you want me to call for you? Family? Friends? I'm sure they would like to know you're here."

"No. There's no one."

"I know what you're going through. Sometimes it helps to have a listening ear."

Oh sure. She thinks she knows everything. How does she know what I did?

"No thank you," she muttered and turned her head away. "You would never understand what I'm going through."

"I won't force you. But I'm here when you're ready. I do want you to know I'll stay as long as you need me."

I wish she would just go away.

"There's someone else here too. Someone who loves you very much. He's waiting for you tell Him everything you feel, about all your hurt and anger. He wants to help you too."

Jerking her head from the pillow, Kari Lynn looked frantically around the room.

"Troy? No, don't let him be here!"

"No, he isn't here. But God is. He wants to help you."

"God doesn't want anything to do with me." She turned her face back toward the wall. "Even if He did, I could never expect anything from Him. Not after what I did."

"I know it seems that way. I thought the same thing after I went through a similar situation three years ago."

Kari Lynn's eyes popped open and she turned back to face the woman.

"You mean you…you've…?" she whispered.

Certainly she hadn't heard right. They would never have someone work in the chaplain's office who did anything as terrible as she did, who had an abortion.

"Yes. It's not something I'm proud of, but if my story helps someone else it's worth telling. If you're willing to listen."

She wasn't sure she wanted to hear the woman's life story, but if she wanted to share it, what could it hurt?

Laura stared out the window for a moment, as if bracing herself against the pain.

"I was very much in love with this young man. He was kind and generous and said he loved me as much as I loved him. I thought he was everything I wanted in a guy, and we planned to be married in another year. One thing led to another, and well, we just couldn't wait. When I found out I was pregnant I didn't know what to do. And of course my young man left the minute he found out. So I was left to face it all alone.

"A friend suggested an abortion and I thought that was the answer. But I was wrong."

A tear slipped down her cheek and she brushed it aside before going on.

"I do know the guilt you feel, because I felt the same way. For months I kept everything inside. Then one day I met someone who told me about Jesus. She said no matter what I did, there is no sin too big or too terrible for Him to forgive.

"When I finally took it all to God, at last I could let go of the pain. Oh, I still regret what I did. I always will, I suppose, but I'm not weighed down with the guilt of it anymore.

"My friends also encouraged me to talk about what I was going through, to not keep it all bottled up inside. And I did. Oh, I'm not saying I broadcast it to everyone, but there were a few close friends I shared with and who prayed with me. It helped me forgive myself."

Laura smiled.

"That's why I'm here with you. I want to help you through this. I volunteer in the chaplain's office to help others — to encourage them to accept God's forgiveness. Once they are able to accept that, then they can forgive themselves and the ones who hurt them. He healed me of all the bitterness. And He wants to do the same for you."

A soft hand touched her arm. Compassion seemed to radiate from the touch.

"Do you mind if we pray?"

"He won't listen to me."

"That's all right. I can talk to Him for you." She patted Kari Lynn's hand, then held it in her own as she bowed her head. "Jesus, You know how Kari Lynn feels right now, how alone and frightened. You love her and want to hold her and wash away all the hurt and guilt. Give her the sense of peace only You can give. Show her how much You love her and long for her to turn to You for comfort."

Kari Lynn's tears could be held back no longer. If only she could have that kind of peace.

But at least she wasn't alone. Others went through the same thing and survived. Maybe she could too.

"If you want to talk, I'm here," Laura encouraged. "If you're not ready, that's fine too. I just don't want you to carry this around for six months the way I did."

Kari Lynn studied the woman for a moment. She did have a kind face, sort of a motherly look about her.

But could she trust her? What she just went through was not something she wanted anyone to know about, especially someone she didn't know. Who knew if this woman would tell everyone what she did?

Yet somehow the compassion this woman seemed to impart drew Kari Lynn toward her. Maybe it wouldn't hurt to share her own story.

"I thought we were in love too," she began slowly. "Although now I wonder if he loved me at all."

The events of the past few months came flooding back as she stared across the room.

"We promised each other we would wait until we were married and thought we were in control. Then one night he didn't want to hold out any longer and convinced me to sleep with him. I knew it was wrong, but I finally consented. That was all it took. After a couple months I found myself pregnant."

She turned away for a moment, took a deep breath, and then went on.

"When I told him, he was shocked and said an abortion was the only solution. We argued about it for a long time. I always knew it was wrong. Even though I tried to tell him it wasn't right, he insisted.

"Then when I said I wouldn't have an abortion, he said he never had any intention of marrying me."

Tears she was unable to stop ran from her eyes as she turned to look at the woman sitting beside the bed.

"Oh Laura, it was awful. I had no idea he felt that way. Finally he told me I'd never have to see him again if I went ahead with it. I felt as though I had no choice. After all, how could I raise a child on my own?"

Tears continued to run from her eyes, soaking her already damp pillow, but they went unheeded.

"After the abortion, the guilt nearly killed me. I couldn't believe I went through with it. It was as though I willing committed...committed murder."

Sobs shook her shoulders.

"I realize now I could have made my own decision. I didn't have to go along with what he wanted. But it's too late now. The damage is done."

She pulled in a deep breath.

"I still can't believe I will never be able to hold a little one in my arms, never know what it's like to feel that first kick. I didn't even carry my baby long enough to experience that."

Her chest heaved with silent sobs she couldn't control.

"I will never be a mother. All because of one mistake. Why, Laura? Why did God let me do such a stupid thing?"

"Don't blame God for what you did. We make these foolish decisions on our own. I did, and so did you. But Jesus isn't condemning you for your decision. He has already forgiven you. And He's ready to take everything — the pain, the guilt, all of it. All you have to do is ask."

If only she could. It would be so wonderful to be rid of the guilt. But how could she ask God to forgive her? No, it was too much.

"I can't. I can't expect Him to forgive me for what I did."

She turned her face toward the wall.

"No one can help me now. Not even God."

chapter 4

Thoughts of Kari Lynn invaded Troy's dreams as he tossed and turned during the night. How was he going to make everything right?

Sunday morning he rolled out of bed, exhausted. But his mind was made up. He would see her today and take the blame for everything.

The future could wait until later.

The short drive to the hospital was spent practicing what he would say. But the moment he stood outside her open door, everything escaped him.

She sat in a chair by the window, her breakfast tray on the table in front of her. It was untouched.

He took a tentative step inside the door. She made no move. He didn't think she was aware of anyone in the room, so he stood looking at her for a minute.

Her shoulders slumped forward in her chair and her long, blond hair hung limp, partially obscuring her face. She stared out the window as though oblivious to anything around her.

It was difficult to resist the desire to rush across the room and take her into his arms. He took a few hesitant steps into the room. He wanted to gather her in his arms, kiss her and tell her how much he loved her, but that would be the wrong thing to do.

"Good morning," he said in little more than a whisper.

When she turned from the window at the sound of his voice, her eyes lit up. A smile began to curve her mouth upward. She started to rise from the chair and he thought she was going to run into the arms he held open toward her.

Then she stopped. As quick as it came, the light in her eyes went out and the smile disappeared. She turned her face away from him.

"What are you doing here?" she asked in a flat voice.

"How are you this morning?"

He took another step toward her.

"You're looking good."

She turned a mocking smile in his direction and tugged at her faded hospital gown. "Oh sure. A regular fashion model."

"I suppose I have seen you look better," he said with a smile.

Another hesitant step.

"But you always look wonderful to me."

"What are you doing here?" This time her voice held an edge.

This wasn't like Kari Lynn, and he didn't know how to take this new behavior.

"Kari Lynn, can you forgive me? I know God has, and it would mean so much if you could."

She sat still, staring at the hands clasped in her lap.

He glanced at the floor and pulled in a deep breath. This was more difficult than he expected.

"I want you to know I take the blame for everything. If I'd listened to you we wouldn't even be here right now. But I'm here for you, I won't abandon you."

Kari Lynn jerked toward him. Fire danced in her eyes.

"Why should I forgive you?" she spat, the sparks in her eyes punctuating her words. "What right do you have coming here after all you did? You told me I mean nothing to you. So what are you doing here?"

He couldn't think of anything to say, although he knew he should give her some kind of answer.

"I thought you loved me," she went on before he had a chance to reply. "But you proved to me you don't even know what love is. How can you stand there and ask me to forgive you?"

The force of her words forced him back a step.

"I do love you," he said softly as he gazed into her eyes. "I always loved you, and I always will. Not for one moment have I stopped loving you."

"Don't lie to me, Troy Hoffman," she shouted, her face contorted with anger. "You told me yourself you never loved me and never intended to marry me."

Tears streamed down her face but she seemed not to notice.

"I was nothing but a play thing to you."

Her words stung as though he was sucker punched. Thoughts failed him for a moment as he stared at her. Shame poured over him. He looked at her several minutes, hoping he could make her understand.

"I suppose I can understand how you might perceive my actions that way," he whispered, "but it isn't the way I meant it. And you're right, that isn't love, not God's kind. But I do love you, Kari Lynn. So much."

Her face softened for a moment before hardening again.

She got to her feet, brushed past him, and fell face down across her bed. Sobs convulsed her body.

"I hate you," she sobbed as she beat her fists into the pillow. "I hate you and what you did to me. Just leave. Don't ever come near me. I never want to see your face again."

He had never seen her this way before and it frightened him. Perhaps coming to see her so soon was the wrong thing to do. Despite what she said, he was tempted to pull her into his arms, yet he knew it would do more harm than good. It was difficult to leave her like this, but he would only make things worse if he stayed.

"I love you," he whispered, then turned and stepped out the door.

Laura was coming down the hall when Troy came out of the room. She seemed surprised to see him.

"How is she this morning?"

"Physically I think she's doing well. But emotionally… well that's a different story. I think it was the wrong thing to do to try to see her this soon. She wouldn't listen or even think of forgiving me."

He scrubbed his face with his hand.

"It hurts so much to see her this way. I know we were wrong. Both of us were. But I know God will forgive us if we only ask."

"I don't think she's able to grasp that concept right now." Her hand patted his arm. "It's all so fresh she can't think straight. She knows what she needs to do, but it's just too much for her to grasp yet. Give her time. She'll come around. But she is going to have to be the one to make the first move. Don't push her. Let her know you are there for her whenever she feels ready to accept you, but it has to be her decision."

He drew in a deep breath and then blew it out in frustration.

"I suppose you're right. I just wish she would let me help

her get through this. Has she talked to you?"

"Yes, some. She's a fighter, I can tell. It was just a hard blow for her and it will take her some time to recover." She turned toward Kari Lynn's room. "I'd better get back to her. But I'll be praying for you both. That's all we can do for now, but God can work miracles. Let's just step back and watch Him work."

"I could certainly use a miracle about now," he said with a lopsided grin. "But yes, I suppose you're right. I guess I'll have to be patient. Something I haven't learned to do very well."

Kari Lynn lay on the bed for some time after Troy left. Thoughts ran rampant through her mind. She couldn't believe he had the nerve to show his face after all the things he told her.

"My life is ruined because of you," she muttered into her pillow. "How dare you come and ask me to forgive you. I can never forgive you. Never!"

Tears that continued to soak her already damp pillow went ignored. Her eyelids were heavy and she couldn't keep them open any longer. It would be a relief to slip away in sleep, away from everything that happened.

A hand touched her arm, waking her with a start. She pulled away from what must be Troy's hand.

"Good morning. You ready to go home?"

She looked up at the sound of a familiar voice. It was a relief to find Dr. Sanderson, her family physician, smiling down at her, not Troy.

Rubbing her sleep filled eyes she pulled herself to a sitting position.

"If you think I'm ready."

The physician thumbed through her medical record.

"Dr. Gordon thinks you are ready to be released. Your blood work looks good this morning, so there's no need to keep you any longer. As long as you feel strong enough to go home. You will need to take things easy for a while. Do you have anyone who can be there with you since you live alone?"

"No, but I'll be fine."

"Are you sure? We can keep you another day if you want."

Dr. Sanderson pulled up a chair next to the bed and settled into it. "Kari Lynn, the next few days are going to be rough for you. You just went through the ringer, physically and emotionally. I'd like for you to have someone to stay with you for the next several days. Someone you can talk to.

"You're ready to go home physically. What happened to you was a shock, not only to your body, but to your emotions as well. I'm not sure you're ready to be by yourself right now. You're sure there isn't someone who could stay with you? One of your friends from church perhaps? What about your Mom? I'm sure she would come from California to be with you."

"I don't want anyone to know what I did." She looked down at the floor. "Especially not my parents. They would be devastated if they knew what I did. And I certainly don't want all our friends to find out. Really, I'll be fine."

"At least you have Troy to check on you. I'll feel better knowing you're not completely on your own."

She drew in a deep breath and looked down at the floor.

"I won't be seeing him anymore."

She hesitated a moment.

"Our relationship is over."

The doctor looked up in surprise.

"He never loved me in the first place and he wants nothing

to do with me now. That's why he insisted I have the abortion, so he could save face before our friends. I guess none of us knew him very well, did we?"

"In that case, maybe I should keep you another day. I don't like the idea of you at home alone."

"No, I would rather go home. I never have liked hospitals all that well, and I'll feel more comfortable in my own apartment. I'll behave myself, I promise." She offered the doctor a weak smile. "I won't try anything stupid this time."

Dr. Sanderson patted her hand as he stood.

"Alright. If you're sure. I'll get your dismissal orders written along with some follow-up instructions. Dr. Gordon will want to see you in his office in a few days to make sure everything is healing properly. If you have any problems or need someone to talk to, don't hesitate to call me. I'm your friend, as well as your physician, you know. You can call me anytime."

When the doctor left she turned her attention to getting out of here. She had no idea where her clothes were, although they were probably ruined anyway.

Even if could find her clothes, she had no idea how she would get home. Maybe a cab? Or the bus? But she wasn't about to be seen out in public dressed like this.

Maybe Troy would help.

As soon as the thought came, she forced it aside. She would never ask him to do anything for her. Not anymore.

There had to be some other way.

She considered calling her friend, Anne. If Anne knew about her situation, she would be here in a minute to help. But she wasn't ready to tell anyone what she did, not even her best friend.

The door opened while she was still trying to come up with a solution and she braced herself for another encounter with Troy. The breath she didn't realize she was holding escaped in a rush when Laura stepped into the room.

"I hear you're dismissed," the woman said in a cheery voice. "Are you ready?"

"Yes, I am. But I haven't figured out how to get there."

"If you need a ride, I could drive you."

"That would be great, but first I have to get dressed. I don't even know where my clothes are."

Laura walked across the room and opened the door of a small closet. She picked up a plastic sack and pulled out some clothes.

"Here they are." She frowned at the bundle she held in her hands. "Is this all you have?"

Kari Lynn nodded.

Shaking her head, Laura held out the bag.

"I don't think you'll be able to wear these. They're still wet. Do you have someone who can bring you some clothes from home?"

"No. No one knows I'm here except Troy. And I'm not about to call him."

"You're sure? He is plenty worried about you. I know he would be glad to help. By the way, that's how I found out about you. He came to our office and asked for help."

Kari Lynn jerked to attention at those words.

"He came to your office?" she snapped. "Who all has he told about this? Do all our friends know? How dare he tell everyone my business!"

"Don't worry." Laura put a hand on her arm. "He didn't say much, but he's hurting too. He needed to talk to someone.

Whether or not you want to believe it, he is concerned about you and wanted to know if there was anyone who could give you some help."

"Ha. He's worried alright." She couldn't keep sarcasm from creeping into her voice. "But not about me. He's just worried about his own reputation."

"I know it's hard to believe right now, but he is genuinely concerned. He spent quite a while in our office."

When Kari Lynn started to object, Laura continued. "Don't be upset. He needed a friend. Someone to talk to. He's affected by this too, you know. But he does want to help."

"Don't let him fool you. He only feels guilty and is concerned about what people will think of him. He doesn't care about me."

Laura turned her attention back to the damp bundle of clothes on the bed. "I can't believe they left your things like this." She shook her head in disgust. "They could have at least hung them up."

She turned to Kari Lynn and smiled. "Well, you can't run around the streets the way you're dressed now. They'd arrest you for indecent exposure. Besides, I think it's a little chilly for that type of attire out there today."

Kari Lynn couldn't help smiling at the woman's attempt at humor.

"Why don't I run to your apartment and bring you something to wear," Laura suggested. "Then when you're ready I can take you home."

"I couldn't ask you to do that. I appreciate the offer, but that's too much to ask."

"That's what I'm here for, to help people. Besides, do you have any better ideas?"

Picking up the cold, damp clothes that lay on the bed beside her, a shiver went up her spine. She couldn't imagine putting them on. She dropped the soggy bundle back on the bed. "I guess I don't have any better idea."

"Then I guess I'm your only alternative." Laura held out her hand. "Why don't you give me your keys? We'll get you out of here so they can't charge you for another day."

Kari Lynn didn't remember if she picked them up when she left her apartment. In fact, she wasn't sure she even locked the door. The only thing on her mind was getting away from everything. After rummaging through the clothes, she was relieved to find them in the pocket of the damp slacks.

She hesitated a moment and finally handed them over.

"I do appreciate this."

"Think nothing of it. That's what I'm here for. Now tell me where you live and what you want me to bring. We'll have you out of here in no time."

❁❁❁

Laura opened the door and ushered Kari Lynn into her apartment.

"I'd like to stop by the next few days and see how you're doing. The doctor said you need someone to help and I would love to be the one to do it."

When Kari Lynn started to protest, she held up her hand.

"I don't mean to intrude. but I wish someone had been there to help me. I know what it will be like the next few days and weeks. You'll need someone, especially since you're not confiding in anyone else right now. I'd like to think we're friends. Maybe I can help you over the rough spots. What do you say?"

A smile came in spite of herself. How could she refuse such a sweet offer?

"I think I'd like that."

"Good! Here's my phone number." Laura handed her a small card. "Call me any time, day or night. I mean it. I can run errands and I've been told I'm a good listener." She grinned and added, "I even make a mean enchilada casserole. Whatever you need."

She opened the door and stepped into the hall.

"I'll stop by again tomorrow. Please try to get some rest now."

Kari Lynn nodded and slowly closed the door behind her new friend. Turning around, she leaned against it and gazed across the room.

She loved this apartment. Despite its small size, she never felt crowded. With its warm colors and large windows it was perfect for her. And she loved the fact that she didn't have to share it with anyone.

Yet, now that she was alone, the walls seemed to close in on her. She was overwhelmed by loneliness.

Attempting to shake off the feeling, she made her way across the room and settled into her recliner. She flipped on the TV and tried to concentrate on the program, but she soon lost interest.

After turning it off, she walked across the room. She stopped to look out the window for a bit, and then began to pace back and forth.

What is wrong with me? I never felt this way before.

When she passed the breakfast bar that separated the kitchen from the living area, she paused. Maybe what she needed was something to eat. After all, she didn't have lunch before she left the hospital and it was now almost two.

She opened a can of her favorite soup, broccoli cheese, and

heated it in the microwave. After only one spoonful and a bite of toast she pushed it away. Leaving it on the counter, she went back to the living room and grabbed the remote.

I just need a good movie.

When she pressed the button a toothless baby grinned as her father played peek-a-boo. She closed her eyes and switched the channel. This time an adorable toddler slurped up food as her mother happily spooned it into her mouth.

There were never this many baby commercials before. Why now? She punched the off button before any more could play.

Would it always be this bad? Laura did say she went through the same thing. Maybe that's why she was so anxious to help.

A frantic search for her friend's phone number finally unearthed it among the hospital discharge papers. She grabbed her phone, dialed the number, but disconnected before the first ring.

"This is ridiculous. I'm not even home an hour and I'm already going out of my mind. I have to stand on my own two feet sooner or later. I may as well start now."

A book she started a few days ago caught her eye and she picked it up. Curling up in the corner of the couch she tried to read. But it was impossible. The words on the page seemed to scream, *Look at you. You call yourself a Christian, but see what you did. God will never forgive you.*

Something Laura said at the hospital echoed in her mind.

There's no sin too big for Jesus to forgive.

Could it be true? She wanted to believe it, but she didn't know if she could. Perhaps God would forgive her for sleeping with Troy, and maybe even for getting pregnant. But He would never forgive her for destroying the life they created that one night.

She shook her head.

"No, that is asking too much."

Frustrated and unable to stand the loneliness of her apartment any longer, she got ready for bed. Maybe if she got some sleep things would be better tomorrow.

As soon as she climbed into bed and closed her eyes, visions of babies with outstretched arms seemed to come at her from every direction. It was hours before a fitful sleep finally claimed her. This must be what it is going to be like from now on.

chapter 5

Kari Lynn sat at her kitchen table attempting to eat breakfast. She loved oatmeal with brown sugar and blueberries, but this morning she could only swallow a couple bites.

The phone rang and she dashed to her bedroom to get it from her night stand. At last, another living soul. It must be Laura. No one else would be calling.

"Hello?"

"Hey. How are you this morning? I went to the hospital and they said you were released yesterday."

Her heart sank at the sound of Troy's voice.

"I thought I made it clear. Everything is over between us."

"But...but..."

She looked at the phone for a moment, and then disconnected it. After staring at it several minutes, she threw it on her bed before trudging back to her uneaten breakfast.

It was difficult to admit to herself, but the call did leave her disturbed. Her pulse had quickened when she heard his voice, just like always. But she needed to forget him now. There was nothing she could do to change the past, and she couldn't risk being hurt again.

"I don't need you, Troy, and I certainly don't need any more of your lies," she muttered as she pushed her spoon through her now cold cereal.

The sound of the dial tone echoed in Troy's ears long after Kari Lynn hung up on him. Her words upset him. He hadn't believed she really meant it when she told him everything was over that day at the hospital. But now hearing her say it again, he realized she was serious.

As difficult as it was for him to accept, it wouldn't solve anything by sitting around the house bemoaning the fact. He still had a job and it was time for him to be on his way.

Once at his office, however, he found it hard to concentrate on his work. He spent more time staring into space wondering how to solve his problems than he did looking at the mountain of papers on his desk. Insurance applications just didn't interest him today.

"Hey, Troy," one of his co-workers called as he stuck his head in the office door. "I'd appreciate a little help here today. People are waiting out front to see someone. What's bugging you, anyway? You seem only half here."

Forcing a smile he glanced at Brad.

"Just a rough weekend I guess. I'm sorry, I didn't realize people were waiting. I'll try to pay better attention."

Brad strolled into the office and perched on the corner of the desk.

"Something bothering you? I noticed the last week or so you aren't your usual self. Trouble in the romance department by any chance?" He flashed his co-worker a sly grin.

"No!" Troy answered, more emphatically than he intended.

His coworker backed away from the desk, his hands in the air. "Sorry. You don't need to take it out on me. I was just asking." He chuckled as he turned to leave the office. "I'm pretty good in that department if you ever need any pointers."

It was a relief when the intercom buzzed to let Troy know one of his clients was here to see him. Perhaps he could get his mind off his problems if he talked to the man. He knew Brad didn't realize how close he came to his dilemma, but there was no way he could share his predicament with him. Or with anyone at work, for that matter. He didn't realize his troubles were so apparent.

At the end of the day he made his way to his car in the office parking lot. He was about to open the door when the pungent aroma of coffee wafted past his nose from the coffee shop next door. It brought with it a memory of Kari Lynn sitting across the table from him in a similar restaurant near her apartment. He could almost see them as they sat, hands clasped, looking into each other's eyes.

He shook his head to clear the image.

But a cup of good strong coffee did sound good about now, after the way his day went. Perhaps if he went here by himself he could get her out of his mind.

His hand was on the door handle when he saw her. She sat alone in the front booth, hunched over a cup of steaming beverage, her back to him. But he would recognize that long, blond hair anywhere. His heart skipped a beat as he jerked the door open.

"Kari Lynn!" he said, louder than necessary.

The woman didn't respond.

He placed a hand on her shoulder and repeated a little softer, "Kari Lynn."

Panic flashed in brown eyes when she turned her head toward him.

He jerked his hand away as though he'd touched something hot.

"Oh, I'm…I thought…" he stammered.

Whirling away, he stumbled toward the entrance. It wasn't her. His face burned with embarrassment as the door swished closed behind him.

"Guess I didn't need that coffee anyway," he muttered as he made his way back toward his car.

The few words he had with Kari Lynn this morning still burned in his memory. It was no use. If that was the way she wanted it then he needed to forget her, forget he ever loved her. It wouldn't be easy.

❁❁❁

The ring of her phone pierced the silence of Kari Lynn's apartment. Her heart skipped a beat when she grabbed for it.

Then she stopped.

What if it was Troy again?

"Don't let it be him," she murmured as she let it ring a few times. Although almost afraid to look, she glanced at the caller ID and saw it was Laura.

"Am I glad you called!"

"Something wrong?"

"Oh, Laura, I don't think I can stand being alone another minute. What's wrong with me? I used to like living by myself." A tear slipped down her cheek and she brushed it away. "Is it normal to feel this way?"

"I called to see if this would be a good time for me to drop by, and it sounds as though it is. Hang on and I'll be right there."

A few minutes later footsteps sounded in the hall. She opened the door just as Laura lifted her hand to knock.

"You said you'd be at the door waiting," the woman chuckled, "but I didn't take you literally."

"I'm just glad you're here," she said as she pulled her new friend toward the couch.

"Been a little rough has it?"

"Rough is the understatement of the year!"

"Care to tell me about it? It does get easier the more you talk about it."

"I don't know how I made it through the last few nights."

She got to her feet and began to pace across the floor.

"I can't sleep. Every time I close my eyes I see tiny babies reaching out to me." Tears rolled down her cheeks. "How long does this go on? I don't think I can take it much longer."

"Every person has a different reaction to the experience you went through. We are all haunted in one way or another, but eventually it does get easier."

"I hope so."

"Have you heard from Troy?"

"He called this morning."

"And?"

"I hung up on him."

Kari Lynn studied her friend for a minute.

"Laura, he told me when he found out I was pregnant he didn't love me. But then he came to the hospital and said he does, he always has. What am I to believe? And if he lied to me once, how do I know he won't do it again? Besides, if he really loved me he would never have insisted on the abortion."

"If you had seen him the night he came to our office you would know he loves you. Anyone could see the man was grieving. Not only for what he put you through, but he was afraid he might lose you. That was more difficult for him than anything. He loves you, Kari Lynn. Trust me."

Kari Lynn chewed on her thumb nail as she paced across the floor a few times.

"I would like to believe he loves me. But even if he does, I don't think I can continue the relationship. Everything is different now."

"It doesn't have to be. Why don't you allow him into your life. Oh, I don't mean you have to continue the relationship you once had right now. But you are both in this together, he's as much a part of everything as you are. And he wants to help. Let him."

"No, Laura, I can't. Just the sight of him or the sound of his voice brings everything back again. No, we're better off both going our separate ways."

Laura didn't reply. She glanced at her watch and then got to her feet.

"I would love to stay longer, but I need to pick up a friend in a few minutes. But I will come by again soon." She started toward the door. "I'm praying for you, asking God to show you His love. He will, you know. He promised."

The door closed and Kari Lynn wandered toward the window. Her friend's words, "He loves you, Kari Lynn. Trust me," rang in her ears as she stared out across the city.

She wasn't sure she believed Laura. How could Troy love her and still do and say the things he did? It didn't make sense.

But the words kept coming back, as much as she tried to ignore them. *If you had seen him you would know he loves you... He was afraid he might lose you... He loves you, Kari Lynn. Trust me.*

As much as she wanted to believe those words, she didn't know if she could. She was confused; she didn't know what to believe anymore.

"Maybe he does love me. He did seem sincere when he came to the hospital. But how can I marry him now after everything that happened No, it would never work."

Yet she hated to give him up. In spite of everything, she thought she did still love him.

As she wandered around her apartment unconsciously straightening things already in place, her mind kept going back to those words: He loves you, Kari Lynn. Trust me.

So he loved her. It would still never work. Not anymore.

She felt a bit better when she woke the next morning. The nightmares weren't quite as bad, and she did feel more rested.

After grabbing a bowl of cereal she plopped down in front of her computer to check the dozens of messages that waited in her email box.

There was one from her mother. The picture she attached of her dad in their rose garden brought a smile to her face. And a tear to her eye when she thought about how much she missed her parents. She clicked on the picture and saved it in her family album file. Before she left the picture folder, her eye caught a glimpse of another file, one marked Troy.

Part of her wanted to delete it. It was all pictures of him and of their time together. But something inside her urged her to open it.

The sight of him nearly took her breath away. Looking at some of the photos brought back so many memories of times they shared during the last two year. Pictures of picnics at the park with friends, concerts, and baseball games - they were all there. Wonderful times full of laughter and tears. They shared an instant connection from the day they met. So much so, she knew their friends were sure it wouldn't be long before they would be married. They were so happy together, and she was sure he was the one God had chosen for her.

Yes, she did miss him. But although she still loved him, she knew they could never go back to the relationship they enjoyed before she got pregnant. She needed to face the new life that now lay ahead of her. A life without Troy.

She bit back tears as she highlighted the file name and typed, 'The Past.' It was time to move on. Looking back was too painful.

With a sigh she shut down the computer.

chapter 6

Somehow Troy managed to keep from calling Kari Lynn the rest of the week. But by Saturday he could hold out no longer. He had to talk to her. Certain she would hang up on him again he decided it would be best to see her face to face.

"Lord, please let her listen to me," he prayed as he rode the elevator up to her apartment.

He stepped off on the twenty-ninth floor, and with a determined stride started down the hall. Still somewhat hesitant, he stood a moment outside her door listening for some sound to indicate she was home. There were voices - probably the TV - so he knocked on the door before he could change his mind.

Wiping his damp palms on the legs of his jeans, he waited for her to answer.

Footsteps came toward the door. His pulse raced.

The door opened and he caught a brief glimpse of her face. She started to close it, but he jammed his foot in the opening.

"Kari Lynn, wait. I need to talk to you."

"There's nothing left to say."

Her eyes were bright with unshed tears. Oh, how he longed to gather her in his arms and soothe away her pain.

Then the door opened wider. He was surprised to see Laura.

"Come on in, Troy. I was about to leave, but now that you're here, you can keep her company."

After a quick glance in his direction Kari Lynn turned to Laura. "Please don't go. I'm sure he won't stay long."

He took a step back. Maybe this wasn't such a good idea after all. It didn't look as though she was happy to see him.

Laura put a hand on Kari Lynn's arm.

"It might be good for you to get things out in the open and try to work them out. Remember, God expects us to forgive others even though it may seem difficult. We can never experience healing unless we are able to forgive those who hurt us."

Kari Lynn backed away from the door. She didn't look at him, just crossed her arms across her chest and muttered, "Okay, but only for a minute."

Laura began to gather her things.

"Kari Lynn needed someone to talk to so I came over, but now that you're here I better be on my way."

She turned to Kari Lynn. "I'll talk to you later. Be sure to give me a call if there's anything I can do for you."

He watched Laura disappear down the hall and then took a few steps into the apartment. Kari Lynn pushed the door closed and walked across the room.

"It's good to see you. How are you feeling?"

She picked up a book and stared at the cover.

"As well as can be expected, I suppose."

Not knowing what to do next, he prayed silently, asking God to help him know where to go from here. It didn't look like it was going to be easy.

He put his hand on her arm. She flinched, but said nothing.

"I have some things I need to say. I hope you'll listen."

She just stared at the book in her hand as if he wasn't even in the room. He waited a moment, wishing she would at least look at him.

Nodding toward the couch, he started in that direction. "Could we go over here and sit down?"

He put his hand under her elbow to draw her across the room, surprised when she didn't pull away.

He lowered himself to the cushions as she dropped into the corner at the other end, her arms crossed across her chest. She stared at a spot on the floor, her face a mask that hid any kind of emotion.

"I understand you aren't happy to see me, but I have some things I need to say."

There was no hint of recognition on her part, so he went on.

"I understand you're upset with me, and you have a right to be. I know I didn't show the kind of love I have for you, and I can only apologize for my behavior these last few months. If I could go back and undo all the things I did to hurt you I would, but we both know we can't change the past. We can only be sure we don't make the same mistakes again in the future."

There was no response.

He prayed for some kind of reaction. Anything, even if it was a fit of anger. There was nothing. Only a stony silence and a blank expression on her face.

"Please look at me."

He moved a few inches closer to her, wishing she would look at him.

She turned her face toward him, but her eyes stared blankly over his shoulder, her finger twisting in the hem of her shirt.

"I may not have the right, but I want to ask for your forgiveness for the things I did to hurt you. My actions were wrong,

I realize that, but I asked God to forgive me. I know He has. It would help if you could forgive me as well."

When he reached for her hand she pulled it away.

"I have missed you so much," he whispered. "My life is empty when you're not there. I need you more than you can ever know."

Kari Lynn shot unexpectedly to her feet.

"You don't need me," she spat through tight lips as she glared down at him. "You told me so yourself."

It felt as though someone suddenly knocked the wind out of him. Apparently she didn't realize he wanted her because he loved her.

He got to his feet and tried to pull her toward him. There was resistance in every muscle.

"I'm sorry for the way I treated you. I know I let things get out of hand. And you're right, that isn't the way God wants us to act. I know we should have waited until we were married, but that's in the past. Today is a new day, we can have a fresh start. Please go on with me from here."

Her eyes brimmed with tears when he looked into her face.

"It's all right to cry," he whispered as he fought back his own. "Perhaps that's what you need."

With hands on her arms, he pulled her gently toward him. Her body was rigid, but her forehead dropped to his shoulder. He longed for her to melt into his embrace the way she used to, though he was grateful she didn't resist him entirely. She seemed on the verge of tears, yet none came. It hurt to see her cry, but he wished she would let them wash away her pain.

Holding her at arm's length, he tipped her head so he could look in her face. There was nothing in her expression to tell him what she was thinking or feeling. If only she would at least let him know how she felt.

"Kari Lynn, say something," he whispered as he held her face between his hands. "Please let me know how you feel. I long for us to be where we were before. I miss you so much. This is so difficult. You never kept things from me before. I know you hurt. But so do I. Tell me what's going on inside. I want to help you get over this ordeal we went through."

She jerked away from him. Taken by surprise, he jumped back.

"Ordeal *we* went through!" she shouted, her face contorted with anger. "I didn't know *you* went through anything so terrible. I didn't see *you* get rid of the baby carried inside your body. I didn't see *your* body destroyed because of someone else's demands. What makes you think *you* went through some terrible ordeal?"

The tears came then. Her shoulders heaved with great sobs. He pulled her into his arms and rubbed his hand across her back. It tore his heart to see the anguish that poured from her soul, but perhaps this was what she needed.

Tears ran down his own face, but he ignored them. Tears not only out of compassion for her feelings, but of remorse for what he put her through and sorrow for the life he forced her to destroy.

"Oh, I know you feel no one could hurt as much as you do. But that baby was part of me as well as you. I feel the pain of it too."

He held her, longing to bury his face in the softness of her hair.

"I'm so sorry," he whispered. "I don't know why I succumbed to those temptations. But I want to go on from here. Please go with me, Kari Lynn. I need you."

After several minutes her shoulders stopped convulsing and the sobs ceased. He lifted her face toward his and wiped her tears with his finger. He smiled through his own.

"You needed that, didn't you?"

"I suppose I did," she replied in little more than a whisper. "It's the first real cry I had since it all happened. I think I do feel a little better."

She reached around him to the table at the end of the couch and picked up a box of tissues. After daubing at the remaining tears on her face she blew her nose. A hint of a smile brightened her face. "I must look terrible."

"You look beautiful." He pulled a tissue from the box for himself. "I don't think I'm in much better shape myself."

Cautious, he took her in his arms again and kissed her forehead. "Can you forgive me for all the things I did to hurt you?"

She pulled away. With her gaze fastened on the floor, she slumped back into the corner of the couch. He gingerly sat down beside her.

Without looking up she spoke, her voice so soft he almost couldn't hear her.

"I don't think I can ever forgive you. I know I should. Laura tells me it's the only way I will ever heal. But I'm sorry, I just can't. There's too much pain."

Tears still made tracks down her face but she seemed to ignore them. He longed to wipe them away, but didn't interrupt her.

"I know you say the baby we destroyed was a part of you, but you can never understand what it's like for me. I carried that little one inside of me. My own lifeblood brought nourishment to the tiny body. When I destroyed that baby my heart was ripped out right along with it. No, I can never forgive you."

He reached for her hand.

"I won't rush you. I understand it will take time for you to forgive me, but I want to be here with you. I want to help you through these rough days."

Without replying she turned away. She got up from the couch and walked behind the recliner, as though to put some distance between them.

"I think it would be best if you left now."

He opened his mouth to say something, but then closed it again. It was obvious he had outstayed his welcome.

He headed toward the door. "Just remember, I'll be here for you whenever you're ready."

Kari Lynn watched the door close behind Troy. Her emotions were in a jumble as she listened to his footsteps disappear down the hall. Part of her was glad to see him go. Another part wanted to run after him and beg him to come back.

"Why do things have to be so difficult?"

As she paced the floor, the picture beside her computer caught her attention. Troy's face smiled back at her and she traced a finger over the warm smile. A tear slipped from the corner of her eye, but she ignored it.

"I have missed the love we used to share. The kind of love that honored God."

She hugged the picture to her breast for a few minutes.

"I just need some time. To think and sort out my feelings."

A piece of paper on her desk caught her attention. She picked it up and started writing.

Dear Troy,

I don't know what to do. Sometimes I want to be with you and other times I think I want you out of my life. I will never be able to give you everything you expect out of marriage. You know I can never give you children. As much as you love them it would never work. I think it would be best for both of us if we went our separate ways.

Tears streamed down her face as she read what she wrote. Then she took the paper in her hand, crumpled it in her hand, and dropped it in the wastebasket.

"Why God, why did You let this happen?"

But she knew the answer. It was her fault, not God's. And as much as she wanted to place all the blame on Troy, she knew she made her own decisions. She was as much to blame as he.

When she turned from her desk the Bible on the end table seemed to stare at her. How long since she last opened the covers?

Is this where everything began? Did we take our eyes off God and think only about ourselves?

The ring of her cell phone interrupted her thoughts. In a way she hoped it was Troy, yet she wasn't sure she wanted to talk to him again. Reluctantly she picked it up without even bothering to check the caller ID.

"Hello?"

"Hi, this is Laura. I'm just calling to see how you are. I know it was difficult to meet with Troy this afternoon. I wanted to make sure you are all right."

"I'm okay."

Although she appreciated her friend's concern, what could she tell her?

"It was hard."

She hesitated a minute.

"He asked me to forgive him for everything."

"And?"

"I can't forgive him. Not yet anyway. I did have a good cry. In fact we both did. It's the first time I really cried since everything happened. It did help some, seemed to ease a little of the pain."

"Any chance the two of you might get back together?"

"I don't think so."

After a long silence Laura asked, "Is that his idea or yours?"

Kari Lynn allowed a loud sigh to escape, releasing with it some of her confusion.

"I can't go back to what we had before. Not right now anyway. It's too difficult."

She sniffed back tears.

"He wants me to forgive him and go on. I know it's what God wants me to do, but I can't. Not yet. I don't know if I will ever be able to do that. And I don't think I can go back to him. Not now, not the way things are. You don't know what it's like to know you can never have children."

"I do know you will to have to forgive him before you can ever heal. Whether or not the two of you go on from here is irrelevant now, but until you are able to forgive him you will always carry your burden of guilt.

"Do you recall the words Paul wrote in the third chapter of Colossians? In verses twelve and thirteen, he says, 'Put on then, as God's chosen ones, holy and beloved, compassionate hearts, kindness, humility, meekness, and patience, bearing with one another and, if one has a complaint against another, forgiving each other; as the Lord has forgiven you so you also must forgive.' Those weren't just words Paul wrote for no reason.

"Then a couple of verses later he tells us, 'And let the peace of Christ rule in your hearts, to which indeed you were called in one body.' So how do you expect to find peace in your life if you don't forgive Troy so that Christ can rule in your heart?

You can't expect Him to abide where there is unforgivness.

"You have to forgive yourself as well. I know what it's like. We blame ourselves for what happened, and we are guilty. But until you come to grips with your own sin and ask God to forgive you, you will never have peace. And you will never be able to forgive Troy. Remember, God has already pardoned you, both of you. That's why He died on the cross, to take our sin as His own. You only need to confess your wrongdoings to Him. Then it's up to you to accept His forgiveness and allow Him to give you the peace He longs to give."

Laura's words struck home as she pondered the words. They were familiar to her, and she did understand what they were saying. She longed for peace, but would God give it to her after what she did? It was difficult to believe He would.

A voice interrupted her thoughts.

"I'm sorry I can't talk longer, but I was anxious to hear how things went with you and Troy. I think you both still love each other. I could tell by the way he looked at you when you opened the door that he loves you. And I believe if you were to tell yourself the truth you would have to admit you love him too. Don't shut him out. You need him now, now more than ever. Even if you never get back together, you still need each other to get through the coming days and weeks."

Yes, she knew what Laura was saying was true; she probably did need someone. And if she was to tell herself the truth, she knew she did still love him.

Forcing her thoughts aside, she turned her attention once again to her friend.

"Thanks for calling. It always helps when I talk to you. I don't know how I would survive if it wasn't for you."

"That's what I'm here for, to help people like yourself and

like me. I'll talk to you again soon. In the meantime, think about what I said."

"I will, and thanks again."

She slipped the phone into her pocket and curled up in the recliner. It was good to see Troy again this afternoon. She did long for him to hold her in his arms the way he did today. Although she had wanted to respond to his embrace, she just couldn't let herself.

Her thoughts turned to some of the things Laura said. Maybe she and Troy did need each other to get through it all. She knew she could never confide in any of her friends from church. Not even her best friend, Anne. They always shared everything with each other in the past, but she couldn't share this. She couldn't even tell her parents.

Except for Laura, there was no one besides Troy. He was the one person she could talk to and who would understand. Like Laura said, even if they never went on from here, maybe they did need each other to be able to survive these rough times. Perhaps it would be good for them to continue to see each other for a while, at least until they had a chance to heal from their wounds.

Although she knew she committed some horrible sins, she also knew God was willing to forgive her if she asked. It was just too difficult to ask Him. She was too ashamed of what she did.

She dabbed at the angry tears that ran down her face as her thoughts turned to what lay ahead for her.

Burying her face in her hands, she wept. It wasn't fair. She always looked forward to the time she would grow up, fall in love, marry a wonderful man, and raise a family. Now those dreams were shattered.

chapter 7

The ring of her phone interrupted Kari Lynn's thoughts. She wondered who it could be this time. Certainly Laura wouldn't call again so soon. In a way she hoped it was Troy, yet she wasn't sure she wanted to talk to him.

"Hello," she said hesitantly.

"Kari Lynn? I hope I didn't disturb a nap or something."

Her pulse quickened at the sound of Troy's voice, in spite of her attempt to not let it affect her.

"No, I wasn't asleep."

"Good, I'm glad I didn't wake you."

He paused a minute.

"We haven't attended church in a long time. I would like to start again. I've missed being with other believers."

When he hesitated she couldn't help wonder why he called. So he wanted to go to church. What did that have to do with her?

"I hoped I could convince you to come with me. Do you think you would feel up to it? I know the surgery and everything was hard on you, but it might be good for you to get out a little."

How should she answer? She was certain she was strong enough, but she didn't know if she wanted to go to church. What would she tell everyone? No doubt they would ask why she wasn't there for so long.

"I don't know. All I've done is lie around the apartment since I came home from the hospital. I'm not sure how strong I am."

"Why don't I come over and we can go for a short walk? Then you can find out."

She chewed on her thumbnail, considering the idea. She wasn't sure if spending time with him was the best thing to do right now. Conflicting emotions chased each other through her mind.

"It would probably be all right. A change of scenery couldn't hurt anything. I am tired of these four walls. And I suppose a little exercise would be good for me."

"Good. I'll be there in fifteen minutes."

Her shoulders rose in a huge sigh and she put the phone back in her jeans pocket. She made her way to the bathroom to freshen up a bit. Maybe this wasn't the best idea. He would most likely get the idea she wanted to continue the relationship. And she didn't know if she was ready for that. At least not yet.

A glance in the mirror revealed dark circles accentuating the puffiness around dull blue eyes. Although she tried to force a smile to her lips, it did little to improve the image. After running a brush through her hair, she turned away from the mirror. No need to worry about her appearance. It wasn't as though she was trying to impress anyone.

Butterflies danced in her stomach when she recognized Troy's characteristic knock. His familiar smile lit up his face when she opened the door. Her pulse raced when she saw him, although she attempted to squelch the effect it had on her.

"You ready?" he asked as he reached for her hand. "You better put on a warm jacket. It's a little chilly out there today."

She turned to get her coat out of the closet. Although she longed for his touch, it was best to keep her distance.

A brisk, autumn breeze blew across her face when she stepped out the door of the building. It felt good after being inside for so long. She took a deep breath and savored the clear, crisp air.

"I think maybe a walk is what I needed," she murmured. "I was tired of doing nothing."

His hand touched hers. A surge of electricity rushed through her and she glanced in his direction. The heat of a blush rushed up her face when she saw him gazing at her. He smiled and closed his hand over hers. She started to pull away, but her heart lurched at the sight of that familiar smile.

Before she realized what was happening, her fingers began to lace themselves between his of their own accord. She looked up and flashed a shy grin. For the moment all the events of the past few months vanished. This was where she wanted to be. With the man she loved.

"Thanks for coming. I was about to go out of my mind in the apartment all by myself."

"I thought it would do you good to get out."

They strolled along the sidewalk for several blocks, stopping once in a while to look at something of interest in some of the shop windows. Neither said much. Just being together was enough.

"Are you okay?" he asked after another block. "I don't want you to overdo your first time out."

"I'm fine."

Actually, just being with him she was more than fine.

"Thanks for suggesting the walk. I think it's what I needed.

But maybe we should start back." She filled her lungs with the fresh air. "As much as I enjoy it out here, we do have to walk the same distance home again, you know. I shouldn't try too much my first time out."

"You're probably right."

He grinned at her and winked, sending that thrill through her.

"I could always carry you back if you're too tired to make it on your own."

"Don't even think about it." She made a face at him. "I would be embarrassed to death."

He chuckled. "All right, I won't embarrass you. This time. We'll just take it easy."

"I'll pick you up at nine tomorrow," Troy said as she unlocked the door of her apartment. "It will be good going to church again. I missed it when we didn't go these last few months. I'm glad to be back where God wants me."

He took her hand in his. His smile sent goose bumps skittering up her spine.

"You look tired. You better get some rest. I'll see you tomorrow. Goodnight, Kari Lynn. Sweet dreams."

He raised her hand to his lips and kissed her fingers, but she pulled away.

"Goodnight. Thanks for the walk."

She stepped inside and pushed the door closed before he could say more. A tremor went through her as she backed against the wall.

"What's happening?" she asked herself. "This can't be right."

Confusion filled her mind. Tonight seemed just like old times.

Yet it could never be the same. Everything was changed now.

Tears welled up in her eyes and slipped down her cheeks. Oh, how she longed for those days in the past when they enjoyed being together. But she might as well get used to the fact a new life lay ahead of her now, not the one she dreamed of so many times in the past.

Overcome by a sudden weariness, she made her way toward the bedroom. She didn't know if she was physically exhausted or if it was the mental strain she was under that made her so tired. Whatever it was, she needed to go to bed.

She slipped out of her clothes, pulled on warm pajamas, and crawled between the covers. Her eyes closed and she waited for sleep to claim her weary body.

Instead of sleep, a battle raged in her mind as she lay staring at the ceiling. The argument with herself kept her awake.

Part of her longed to be in Troy's arms.

Yet another part screamed, *Don't trust him. Look at what he did to you already. You can't let him hurt you any more than he has already.* As hard as she tried to pray, her prayers seemed to go no further than the tip of her tongue. Tears of anger and frustration soaked her pillow as she called out to God.

"Where are You?" she sobbed. "Why did You let all these things happen to me? I thought You were supposed to be there for me. So now where are You when I need You?"

There was no answer. He must have left her to face her problems alone.

She sobbed bitter tears and continued to cry out to a God who didn't answer. A God she turned her back on the last few months.

A sudden noise woke her from a sound sleep. Not fully awake, she groped for the ringing cell phone on the nightstand.

"'Lo," she muttered.

"Oh, were you still asleep? I'm so sorry; I didn't mean to wake you. I probably shouldn't have called so early."

"Is that clock right? Is it almost eight already? I can't believe I slept this late!"

She threw back the covers and stumbled across the room, covering the yawn stretching her mouth with her hand.

"I'm glad you did call, Laura. I guess I forgot to set the alarm before I went to bed last night. It's past time for me to get up."

"Good. I'm glad I didn't wake you needlessly. I'm sorry to be so late in asking, but I wondered if you would like to go to church with me today. Do you think you feel up to it?"

"Oh, I'm sorry. I wish you had asked earlier. Troy called last evening and asked me to go to our church with him."

If she didn't hurry she would never be ready when he came, so she took advantage of the phone in her hand and went to her closet to find something to wear. Another yawn snuck up on her and she attempted to stifle it as she shuffled through her clothes.

"I don't know why I consented to go with him. I don't look forward to meeting all our friends."

A sudden thought hit her. Her hand flew to her mouth and the blouse in her hand dropped to the floor.

"What will I tell everyone when they ask where I was? None of them know what happened. I know they all wonder why I wasn't in church. Troy and I never missed unless we were sick or out of town. At least not until we started doing those things we were ashamed of. What can I say to them? I didn't think of that when he asked me. There's no way I can go."

She chewed on her thumbnail debating what she should do.

"Maybe I should call and tell him I changed my mind. I didn't get much sleep last night, and I am pretty tired. Perhaps I should stay home."

"Kari Lynn, you will have to face your friends sooner or later. The longer you wait to tell them where you were, the more difficult it will be. You don't need to go into detail. We all make mistakes. You'd be surprised how supportive people can be when we have difficulties."

"You make it sound so simple. I wish it was that easy."

"You'll see. If they are true friends they'll understand."

Neither spoke for a minute.

Finally Laura broke the silence.

"So, are the two of you back together? I prayed you might come to realize how he feels about you."

"No, not really. I don't know why I consented to go with him this morning." She pulled in a deep breath. "He said he would be here at nine, so I suppose I better get ready."

Thinking about what was ahead, tears came to her eyes.

"Oh Laura, I don't want to go. I can't. There's no way I can face those people and all the questions they will ask."

"Yes you can. Remember, you're not alone. God is with you."

"I'm not so certain about that. It seems He's forsaken me."

"No, I think it's the other way around. I think it's you who turned away. He's still waiting for you to come to Him."

She was still hurrying to get ready when Troy's familiar knock sounded at the door. For a minute she considered ignoring him. But she knew he wouldn't give up easy. Feet dragging, she shuffled across the apartment.

"Morning," he greeted her when she opened the door. He flashed a bright smile. "You ready to go?"

"Not quite. I'm afraid I got up a little late. Why don't you go on without me? It will take me a while yet."

"Shouldn't take long. You look great the way you are."

He took a step toward her and pushed the door closed behind him.

"Did you get some rest last night?"

The concern in his eyes was almost her undoing, although she tried her best to ignore it. He didn't need to fret over her; she was none of his concern.

"Do you feel all right?"

He put his hand on her arm, causing a tingle to run through her, although she tried to shove the feeling aside. She wanted to tell him she didn't feel strong enough to go anywhere this morning, but she knew it wasn't the truth.

"I am a little tired." She pulled in a deep breath. "I can't seem to get a good night's sleep anymore. You don't have to wait for me. I don't want to make you late. I still have to curl my hair and brush my teeth."

"I'll wait."

He started toward the living room, apparent he had no intention of leaving.

"I'll hurry," she muttered.

Laura's words echoed in her ears as she stalked toward the bathroom. *You will have to face your friends sooner or later. The longer you wait to tell them where you were, the more difficult it will be.*

But she couldn't tell anyone where she was the last few months. She would probably be turned out of the church if they knew everything she did.

The feel of Troy's touch still skittered up her arm as she rolled the curling iron up a strand of hair. She tried to force it away, but to no avail.

Why does he still affect me this way? There can never be anything between us now.

Scowling at her reflection, she tapped her foot as she waited for the last curl to heat up.

"You look terrible," she grumbled to the image in the mirror. "Everyone will know something is wrong and ask all kinds of questions. How do you intend to answer them?"

She picked up her toothbrush and toothpaste, flipped the cap off and squeezed paste on the brush. In her frustration she used too much force and a large glob fell in the sink.

"Why do I even want to go?" she asked around furious strokes of the brush. "God and I aren't on the best of terms lately, so why do I want to pretend everything is all right between us? Nothing like being a hypocrite."

After rinsing out the toothbrush she threw it back in the holder and then brushed out her long curls.

"That's the best you can do with what you have," she told the reflection in the mirror as she took one last look.

Troy smiled when she stepped into the living room.

"Ready? You look great."

Before she could stop him, he tilted her chin and planted a kiss on her lips. She attempted to ignore him, yet she did long for more. Moving toward the door, she picked up her keys from the table.

"We better go," she said without looking at him. "We'll be late enough as it is."

He took them from her hand and guided her out the door,

locked it and dropped the keys in his pocket. With an arm around her waist he led her toward the elevator.

"Please don't do that," she said as she pushed his arm away.

The door opened and she stepped inside, nodding to the two passengers already on board. She avoided Troy's eyes. He would never understand.

She felt his gaze on her as they rode the elevator. It sent a tingle rushing up her spine, but she ignored it the best she could.

A crisp, autumn breeze hit her as soon as she stepped out the door. Goose bumps rose on her arms and she shivered.

"Cold?" His arm went around her shoulders.

She pulled away and wrapped her arms around herself.

"I suppose I should have worn a jacket."

"Want to go back and get one?" He turned toward the door.

"No, we're late enough already. I'll be all right."

❁❁❁

Kari Lynn breathed a sigh of relief as she and Troy slipped into seats in the back row of the Sunday school class. The lesson had already started and she silently rejoiced. At least she didn't have to answer a lot of questions, although she knew the time was coming when she wouldn't be able to avoid them.

"Glad to see you, Troy and Kari Lynn," the teacher said as he looked in their direction. "We've missed you."

"I'm happy to be back, Chuck," Troy responded.

Friends turned and waved a greeting. She forced a half-hearted smile to her lips and lifted her hand in the semblance of a wave. By the expression on their faces it was obvious they were full of questions, and she hoped she could slip out at the end of class the way they came in and avoid having to talk to anyone.

The topic of the morning was forgiveness, something she knew she should pay attention to. But with her mind consumed with thoughts of all the questions she knew were coming, she was unable to concentrate on the lesson.

The sound of Troy's voice next to her interrupted her thoughts. "I came to experience God's forgiveness in my life first hand recently."

Everyone turned to listen to what he had to say. She slid down in her seat trying to make herself invisible, wishing she never came. Certainly he didn't intend to tell everything!

"I've not been here the last few months because I found myself involved in some things I shouldn't."

Face burning with embarrassment, she stared at the hands in her lap. Although she didn't dare look, she knew every eye in the room was on her. If she knew Troy planned to tell everyone what they did, she would never have agreed to come with him.

His voice was strong as he went on.

"I suppose I was ashamed of my actions and that's why I wasn't here. But recently I came to know God's forgiveness in a way I never quite experienced before. It's wonderful to realize the words of First John one verse nine do work. 'If we confess our sins, he is faithful and just to forgive us our sins and cleanse us from all unrighteousness'. I know there is no sin so big that God will not forgive us."

"I'll second that," Chuck agreed. "I know we all find ourselves there at one time or another and know what you're saying."

Certainly Troy didn't plan to say more. She didn't realize she was holding her breath until it escaped in a rush when everyone focused their attention once more on Chuck and the lesson. Troy's hand covered her own and she allowed herself to relax.

The moment class was over she found herself surrounded by friends. She looked around for some means of escape. Troy seemed to want to stay and talk, and before she had a chance to slip out, Anne's arm went around her.

"I've missed you lately. Were you out of town? I tried to call several times but you never answered."

"I…I wasn't well. I'm just now getting my strength back."

It wasn't exactly a lie.

"Why didn't you let us know?" Crystal asked. "We would have prayed for you."

"I…I guess I didn't think of it."

She looked down at the floor.

"If you will excuse me, I think I'll go to the sanctuary."

She tapped Troy's arm. "Could we please go sit down? I feel a little weak."

"Of course."

He excused himself from the group of men. When she felt his hand on her elbow she wanted to push it away, but thought that would foster more questions in their friends' minds. She felt his gaze on her as he guided her out of the room, but she kept her eyes straight ahead.

"Are you all right?" he asked when they stepped into the hall. "We can leave now if you want. I don't want you to overdo."

"No, I'm okay. I just needed to get away from all the questions. I knew they would start to ask what kind of illness I had and I didn't know how to answer."

"I understand."

His arm went around her waist as they made their way past people in the halls. She flinched, but didn't comment. Several called to them as they passed and she was aware of Troy nodding or waving in acknowledgment. She was thankful he kept on toward the sanctuary instead of stopping to talk, the way he usually would. Although she was uncomfortable with him so close, she did appreciate his concern and was grateful he understood how she felt.

The entire morning seemed planned for her benefit. When she glanced through the worship bulletin, she saw the title of the morning message. Forgiveness - Is it necessary?

First the Sunday School lesson, and now the sermon. She glanced out of the corner of her eye at Troy. Did he know the topic of the lessons and that's why he wanted her to come to church with him?

Several verses hit a tender spot when the pastor read the text from Matthew and Mark. They recorded the time when Jesus spoke to his disciples about the importance of forgiving those who wronged them. If they refused to forgive others, they couldn't expect their Heavenly Father to hear them when they asked for His forgiveness.

Oh, God, is this why my prayers don't seem to go anywhere? Is this why You brought me here today? I know I need to forgive Troy. It wasn't entirely his fault. I'm as much to blame as he is. At least the surgery was none of his doing. Lord, I know I grieved You. I would like to ask You to forgive me for the things I knew were wrong, but I can't believe You are willing to do that. And I know I should forgive Troy, but it's too hard. I don't know if I will ever be able to forgive him.

chapter 8

When Troy suggested he take her to one of their favorite restaurants after church, Kari Lynn consented. Although she knew she shouldn't spend so much time with him, she wasn't ready to completely give up his company.

Even though it was one of her favorite meals, she found herself merely pushing the food back and forth on her plate. The verses the pastor read during the morning message still rang in her ears.

For if you forgive others their trespasses, your heavenly Father will also forgive you, but if you do not forgive others their trespasses, neither will your Father forgive your trespasses.

If those verses said what she thought they said, she couldn't expect God to hear her if she refused to forgive Troy. It was a lot to think about.

"What's the matter, Kari Lynn?"

Her mind elsewhere, she jumped, her fork slipping from her fingers and clattering on her plate.

"Was this morning too much for you? Maybe I should take you home"

Closing her eyes, she drew in in a deep breath before pulling away from the hand covering hers.

"I suppose I am tired," she murmured, "although I didn't do enough this past couple of weeks to wear me out. I guess I didn't realize how weak I still am."

"If you're finished eating, why don't I take you home? I don't want you to overdo your first time out."

Out of the corner of her eye she noticed him nodding toward her plate of barely touched food as he said, "You should try to eat something."

She picked up her fork and speared a tiny piece of chicken, forcing herself to put it in her mouth and chew.

"Are you eating at home? You need decent meals if you want to bounce back the way you should."

She winced when he reached out his hand and tilted her chin.

"You aren't eating, are you?"

"I fix myself meals," she muttered and turned away to stare across the room.

"Do you eat them? It doesn't do any good to fix food if you don't eat any more than you have today. I know all of this is hard on you, but you need to take care of yourself. Do you have anything to cook in your apartment? If you need something from the store I'll be glad to go for you. Don't be afraid to ask for help if you need it."

She slid a few kernels of corn on her fork without looking at him. "I have plenty of food. I don't get hungry when I don't do anything all day."

"How about if I stop by when I get off work in the evening and cook you a good meal? I wouldn't mind a little company?"

"No!"

Realizing she'd shouted, she lowered her voice. "That won't be necessary. I make meals for myself, at least all I need for the amount of exercise I get. Laura already volunteered to go to the store for anything I need. And I should get out a little more this week if I intend to get my strength back."

Even without looking, she knew Troy's gaze rested on her, but she refused to look at him.

She pushed herself away from the table.

"We better go. I am pretty tired."

When Troy put his hand under her elbow to guide her toward the door, she forced herself to step away from the touch.

The drive home was a quiet one. Although Troy made several attempts to start a conversation, she didn't feel like talking. To anyone.

As soon as the car stopped she opened her door and stepped out. When she saw Troy start to get out, she held up her hand.

"No need for you to see me to my door. I'm tired and I just need to go in and get some rest. And knowing you," she added with a forced grin, "you will want to stay all afternoon and talk."

She started up the walk to the apartment building, but then turned back toward the car.

"Thanks for lunch," she called over her shoulder. "It was nice to get out of the apartment for a while."

The outside door was about to close behind her when she saw Troy jump from the car and dash up the sidewalk. She wondered what he wanted now. Couldn't he understand she wanted to be alone? He burst through the door as she was about to step into the elevator.

"You might want these."

Her keys jingled in his outstretched hand.

She held the elevator door open and took them from him.

"Thanks. I forgot you took them this morning," she murmured, then let the door slide closed between them.

Troy shook his head as the elevator door swished shut. He turned and made his way toward his car. She was never this distant before. He thought she enjoyed his company when they went for the walk last night, but today was a different story.

He sighed and turned the key in the ignition. He supposed it would take time for her to get over what happened and he needed to learn to be patient. But it was difficult when he wanted to be with her so much.

After one more glance toward the windows of her apartment, he backed out of the parking space and turned toward the street.

"I'll win you back again, you'll see," he whispered. "I am not giving up that easy."

Concern for Kari Lynn was Troy's constant companion all evening. She hadn't seemed herself today. He considered calling her but decided against it. At least for now. If she was as tired as she tried to make him believe, he would let her rest. He could check on her tomorrow.

After a restless night's sleep he picked up his phone. He needed to make sure she was all right. When he dialed her number he was surprised when it went to voicemail. Staring at the instrument in his hand he waited for her greeting to end.

"Good morning, Kari Lynn," he said after the beep. "I hoped to hear your cheery voice, but you must still be asleep. I wanted to check and see how you feel this morning. You do need a little extra rest, but if you are there I would like to talk to you."

There was no reply.

He tried to tell himself she was probably still asleep since she told him yesterday she was tired, although he was certain she only used that as an excuse to be left alone. He'd call again later.

Before leaving for work he decided to try once more to reach her, surprised when the call again went to voicemail. Certainly she should be up by this time. He slowly disconnected the phone.

Several times at the office he tried to call her. It always went to voicemail. Concerned by this time, he decided to drive to her apartment when he got off work.

It took forever for the elevator to reach to the twenty-ninth floor. Or so it seemed anyway. His stomach churned as he made his way down the hall to her apartment. Thoughts of that day in the park when she passed out in his arms raced through his mind, causing his anxiety level to escalate. He couldn't ignore the feeling he would find something he wasn't prepared for when he got to her apartment.

He knocked on the door several times. There was no response.

"Kari Lynn, are you all right? Please answer."

Worry that something happened to her again refused to be squelched. Something didn't feel right. He raised his hand and knocked once more. Was she just ignoring him, or was something wrong?

"Are you all right?" he called, his mouth close to the edge of the door. "At least let me know you're okay, then I'll leave you alone."

With his ear glued to the wooden slab, he listened for any sign of movement. Not a sound. He turned and started back toward the elevator.

As hard as he tried, he was unable to shove the thought from his mind that something wasn't right. Visions of all kinds of things that could happen to her floated through his mind. He almost lost her once and he hoped she wasn't. . .

But he couldn't go there. At least not yet.

When he stepped outside he noticed her car wasn't in its usual spot. He swiveled his head back and forth scanning the parking lot. It was nowhere.

She probably had a doctor's appointment. He shouldn't panic.

Although he tried to set his mind at ease, his conscience wouldn't let him rest. Even if she had a doctor's appointment, he should have caught her at home one of the times he called.

Maybe she went to see Laura. He would call her when he got home and see if she heard from Kari Lynn.

As soon as he got to his apartment he tore through the papers cluttering the top of his desk to find the card Laura gave him with her phone number. Finally he found it in his jacket pocket and dialed the number.

"Hello, this is Laura."

"Troy Hoffman. Have you heard from Kari Lynn lately? I tried several times to contact her, but she doesn't seem to be home."

"No, we haven't talked since yesterday morning. Why, is something wrong?"

"I don't know. I tried several times to reach her by phone, but all I get is her voicemail. I went past her apartment after work and she didn't answer the door. And I didn't see her car in the parking lot. I can't figure out where she could be."

Overcome by worry, he let his forehead drop into his hand.

"You don't suppose something happened to her do you? I thought she was all right, although she did tell me yesterday she was pretty tired. But when I didn't see her car I wondered where she could be."

"That does sound unusual. Let me check around a little and I'll get back with you. I'll try to call her myself. I know she usually checks the caller ID before answering and only picks up the ones she wants to talk to. She always answers when I call. I'll see if I can get her to respond."

"Thanks. I appreciate it. I don't know what I would do if anything happened to her."

"Now don't start thinking the worst. I'm certain there is a logical explanation. I'll get back to you as soon as I find out anything."

Troy sat with his phone in his hand waiting for Laura's return call. When his stomach rumbled he realized it was past dinnertime. It might take some time for her to find out anything, so he started toward the kitchen.

After popping a TV dinner in the microwave, he sat staring at the phone on the table, willing it to ring with some good news.

Even though he was waiting for the call, he still jumped when it rang. A forkful of peas spilled onto the floor.

"Troy, this is Laura."

His pulse sped up.

"Did you find her?"

"No, I didn't get any answer either. I even checked at the hospital she was in before, just in case, but she wasn't admitted. I don't know where she could be. Do you know anywhere she might go? Her family is a long way from here, I believe, and she told me she didn't want any of her friends to know what happened. You know her better than I do. Do you suppose she did go visit one of them?"

"I can't imagine who it would be. I'm sure she wouldn't go

to see her parents. They live way out on the West Coast. I hope she didn't attempt to drive that far, no stronger than she is."

He ran his fingers through his hair trying to think of some place she could be.

"We do have a lot of friends in town, but I know she didn't want any of them to find out what happened. I can't imagine she would go to see any of them. In fact, when we went to church yesterday she didn't want to stay and talk with anyone. She was afraid she would have to tell them what happened. It's unlikely she would go to see any of them. She does have one close friend, but I don't think she even talked to her lately."

"Could you call some of them, perhaps her close friend, in case she might decide to confide in her?"

"I really hate to. She was adamant we not let anyone know what went on between us and about the abortion. I'm afraid if I start to call around to look for her, they'll ask questions." He ran a weary hand across his face. "I think I'll wait on that until we explore all the other possibilities. I don't want to do anything that could widen the gap that already exists between us."

"That is probably wise."

He heard a loud sigh before Laura went on. "I'm at a loss where to go from here. Can you think of any other place she could possibly be?"

"None I can think of right now."

He dropped back into the chair, slouching in frustration.

"I suppose I just need to wait for her to contact me. Thanks anyway for your effort."

"I'm sorry I couldn't be more help. Let me know if you hear anything. I'll keep checking and see if I can get hold of her. Rest assured I will be in prayer for her. For both of you."

"Thanks. I appreciate it. I'll let you know the minute I know anything."

After disconnecting the phone he went to the window and stared out into the dark night. This wasn't like Kari Lynn. He couldn't push aside thoughts that something dreadful happened to her.

Visions of her collapsing in his arms in the park continued to race through his mind. He hoped there wasn't some other kind of complication. Maybe it was the wrong thing to do to encourage her to go out yesterday so soon after surgery. She wasn't all that strong yet.

The fact that her car wasn't in the parking lot caused even more concern. Perhaps she was in an accident. He would never forgive himself if anything happened to her now.

When he realized there was nothing more he could do, he took his problem to the Lord. Something he should have done in the first place. If anyone could help him find her, God could.

In the midst of his petition to God for His help a thought flashed through his mind. Why didn't he think of it before? He had a key to her apartment! The one she gave him after she locked herself out, just in case it happened again.

"Thanks for that reminder, Lord."

Papers and pens flew in the air as he rummaged through his desk. When he finally found it in the back of the top drawer, he snatched it and dashed to his car without even stopping for a jacket. Certainly her apartment would give him some answers.

Screeching to a stop in front of her the building, he sprinted across the parking lot and in the door. He paced in front of the elevators, certain they had stopped running. When one of the doors finally opened he jumped in and punched the button for the twenty-ninth floor. The car stopped and he pushed past the half open door, hitting his shoulder in the process.

"Ouch, that smarts!"

But he didn't slow his pace. Rubbing his shoulder he dashed down the hall to Kari Lynn's apartment.

Before putting the key in the lock, he paused. He wasn't comfortable barging in on her if she was home and maybe asleep.

He lifted his hand and knocked. There was no response.

"Kari Lynn, are you there?"

There was no answer so he knocked once more. Still no reply.

He glanced at the key in his hand and breathed a prayer for wisdom before inserting it in the lock, hesitating again before turning it. A strange foreboding enveloped him.

chapter 9

Troy opened the door an inch or two.

"Kari Lynn?"

Not hearing anything, he opened the door wider and switched on the light. Everything looked okay so far.

Going to the bedroom last, he hoped he would find her there sound asleep.

"Kari Lynn?" he called again before turning on the light.

Everything appeared normal. The bed was made and there was no sign of anything amiss.

That's when he noticed her cell phone on the nightstand. That was unusual. She never went anywhere without it. He picked it up. The icon indicating several voicemail messages caught his eye. Maybe he would find his answer there, although it was unlikely.

He stared at the phone a moment before going to the voicemail folder. Now if he could just think of her password. Then it hit him. He chuckled, recalling the day she laughed and told him she was using "cute." It fit her.

There were several messages, both his and some of Laura's. Finally he came to an unfamiliar number. He pushed the button to listen.

"This is your mother. You're dad and I don't think it's a good idea for you to go up to the cabin. I'm sure it must be cold up there by now. I know we have the fireplace, but I don't think there was much wood left the last time we were there. You didn't plan to go alone did you? It's pretty remote up there, you know. Well, hope you get this message before you leave. Call us back and let us know what you decide."

"The cabin?" He shook his head. "Why would she go to there?"

The two of them spent a weekend at the Moore's lake cabin when her parents came for a few weeks last summer, and it was indeed in an isolated area. He didn't like the idea of her up there alone. Not at this time of year, when everyone else would be gone for the winter.

Maybe he should drive up to make sure she was okay, but then he realized he didn't remember how to get there. And since he didn't know the exact address of the cabin, his GPS would be of no help at all.

He scratched his head. Maybe he could call her parents and get directions. But what could he give for a reason for going? Well, he'd just have to think of something once someone answered.

The next question was how to get hold them. Surely she would have them in her contact list. Sure enough, there was one labeled Mom and Dad. He pressed the icon.

Doubts began to cloud his mind. As he listened to the phone ring, he wondered if he was doing the right thing. Certainly they would wonder why he didn't know where she was. Maybe this wasn't such a good idea after all. He was about to hang up when someone answered.

"Hello."

"Mrs. Moore?"

"Yes."

"This is Troy Hoffman. Kari...Kari Lynn's friend."

"Troy, how nice to hear from you."

She hesitated a moment then asked, "Is something wrong? She called last evening and asked if anyone was using the cabin, said she planned to go there. I'm surprised you didn't go with her."

"I'm afraid we're not on the best of terms right now."

"I'm sorry to hear that. We thought the two of you were getting along so well. In fact, we expected to hear of wedding plans before long. Anything serious or just a lover's quarrel?"

"I'm not sure exactly."

He breathed a sigh of relief. At least so far he didn't need to divulge anything. It was up to Kari Lynn to tell her parents what happened. He would never destroy her confidence.

"I think she just needed to get away from the city for a while. Anyway, I called to get directions to the cabin."

What reason could he give for going there if the woman asked?

"I hate to see her there by herself this time of year and thought I would go up and check on her. But I'm afraid I don't remember how to get there. I know it would be easy to get lost in that wilderness."

"Yes, it would. I'm glad you're going. We hated to think of her up there in that remote area right now too. This time of year everyone has closed up their cabin and no one is around."

She hesitated a few seconds before adding, "That must be some spat the two of you had if she felt she needed to get away to the cabin."

"We aren't quite seeing eye to eye at the moment, but I hope it will blow over. I am concerned about her up there. The weather has turned pretty cold here lately, and I'm sure it's even colder up in the lake area."

"I'm sure she'll be okay. We keep plenty of blankets at the cabin and there's a fireplace in case it gets that cold. I wouldn't worry about that. She knows what the weather is like up there so I'm sure she took plenty of warm clothes with her."

He couldn't tell Mrs. Moore that her daughter recently had surgery and wasn't fully recovered yet. That would only encourage more questions he wouldn't be able to answer.

As she gave directions he jotted them on a scrap of paper he found in his pocket.

"We did think it strange she wanted to go up there by herself, but she seemed in a hurry to be on her way so we didn't talk long. I thought it unusual she would go on a Sunday evening, though. That's an odd day to go somewhere that far away. Didn't she have to work this week?"

"I guess she decided to take some time off." He chuckled. "Probably to get away from me for a while."

So far, so good. He wouldn't destroy Kari Lynn's confidence if he could possibly help it.

"Well, I better go. Thanks for the directions."

"I hope everything works out between the two of you. Tell her she better hang on to you. She couldn't find a better man for a husband as far as we're concerned."

"Thanks. I'll be sure to tell her."

He chuckled as he disconnected the phone. It was good to have someone from her family in his corner.

After slipping the piece of paper with the directions in his pocket, he started toward the door. He wondered how long she planned to stay. It was too far to drive just for the evening.

Then he remembered when he first came to the apartment he noticed her toothbrush and toothpaste on the bathroom vanity. Certainly she wouldn't go to stay overnight and not take those things with her. Or her cell phone. He checked the closet by the door. As far as he could tell it didn't appear she even took a coat. If she didn't take a jacket she probably didn't take anything else with her.

It was uncomfortable snooping around the apartment when she wasn't there, but if she didn't at least take a coat and a change of clothes with her, he better take a few things for her. She would need them if she intended to stay any time as all.

Rummaging in her closet, he found a small suitcase. He knew she would be upset when she learned he went through her personal things, but he couldn't think about that now. After packing what he thought she might want, he picked up the bag and left her apartment.

A cold wind hit his face when he stepped out of the building. A shiver scuttled through him and he thought about Kari Lynn. He knew it was even colder at the lake than here in the city, and he hoped she was warm enough. She didn't need anything to interfere with her recovery now.

If she didn't take the bare essentials with her, she probably didn't take anything to eat either. Stores wouldn't be open up there this time of year, so as soon as he returned to his apartment he went to the kitchen and packed a box of food to take with him.

When he glanced at his watch he decided he better call Laura before it got any later. He knew she would still be concerned.

"I hope she's all right," she said when she heard the news. "I would appreciate it if you could let me know how she is when you find her. I'm glad you're going. I know it is pretty remote in some of those areas, and I would hate for something to happen to her there alone."

"That's what I thought. I'll keep you informed if I can, although I don't know how much cell phone reception there is up there. If I'm able, I'll let you know how she is when I find her."

"I'd appreciate that. When do you plan to leave?"

"It's pretty late to go anymore tonight. It's a several hour drive if I remember right. Besides, I need to get some things together yet so it would be a while until I could be on the road. I'm sure she would be in bed long before I got there, and I wouldn't want to frighten her if I came in the middle of the night. I think it would be best if I went in the morning. Besides, I need to let them know at work I won't be in for a few days."

The blare of the alarm clock jolted him awake with a start the next morning. He rolled out from under the covers and rubbed his sleep filled eyes. If he intended to get to the cabin today he better get a move on.

Anxiety haunted him and he continued to worry. He realized that would not help the situation, so he paused to turn everything over to his Heavenly Father. It was hard to tell what condition he might find Kari Lynn in when he got there, but he could only hope she would be all right.

The road to the cabin seemed longer than he remembered. The cabins nestled among the trees all appeared to be closed up for the season. In spite of his attempt to leave everything in the Lord's hands, worry continued to consume his mind.

He understood why she might choose to come to such an isolated place, even this time of year. It was peaceful here. It would be a good place to try to think things through.

Before getting out of the car he sat for a moment and looked around. Memories of that weekend he spent here with Kari Lynn and her parents came to mind. His eyes wandered to the cabin nestled at the edge of the forest. The light green walls with darker green shutters blended nicely into the trees surrounding it. Noticing the chairs on the porch, he smiled when he remembered the evening he and Kari Lynn sat watching fireflies blink their lights on and off above the grass. The rowboat turned upside down on the sand beside the dock brought back memories of the afternoon he took her out in the boat. He could still almost feel the warm sun on his back as he lazily rowed across the calm lake, watching her trail her fingers in the water, nearly asleep in the bow of the boat.

He shook his head to bring his mind back to the present. He wasn't here to reminisce; he was here on a mission. The quicker he started to look for Kari Lynn, the sooner he would know if she was safe.

As he stepped out of his car he noticed all the shutters on the cabin windows were closed. It looked deserted. And he didn't see her car anywhere. Maybe she didn't come after all. Or perhaps she left already. It didn't seem she came prepared to stay.

Something partially hidden in the trees along the side of the building caught his attention. He quickened his step in that direction.

Her car! She is here.

He sagged against the porch a moment, then made his way to the front of the cabin. Although everything looked deserted, she had to be here since her car was. Only one way to find out. Lifting his hand he knocked on the door.

There was no answer.

He rapped again.

Still no reply.

He put his ear to the door to listen for any movement.

There was nothing.

"It's me, Troy. May I come in?" he called.

Worry he tried to contain prickled up his spine.

He tried the knob, surprised when it turned, and pushed the door open a crack.

"Kari Lynn, are you here?"

Silence.

The only sound was the wind sighing through the pines and waves lapping on the shore.

He stepped inside and looked around. From the musty smell of the place, it appeared no one occupied it recently. The fireplace looked as though it was used not long ago, but when he put his hand on the partially burned logs there wasn't even a hint of warmth.

As he looked around the room he couldn't help remembering the weekend he spent here with Kari Lynn and her parents. He dropped into the soft, tweed cushions of the one of wood frame chairs. A smile came to his lips when he thought of the four of them settled in the rustic couch and chairs clustered around the native rock fireplace. Her parents had accepted him like one of the family, and he felt so at home with them. The weekend had gone by much too fast.

But he wasn't here to remember days gone by. He had to find Kari Lynn. He checked the refrigerator and some of the cupboards at the other end of the room. Apparently she hadn't brought anything to eat. The fridge wasn't even cold. Good thing he brought something with him.

The bedrooms were at the back of the cabin. He took a few cautious steps, hoping he would find her asleep in one of them.

When he opened the door of the first bedroom he could tell it wasn't occupied recently. The bed was neatly made, but a layer of fine dust covered the top of the chest. He picked up a

Western novel that lay open on the nightstand, apparently one Mr. Moore was reading last time he was here. Putting it back, he left the room and went to the next one.

This one appeared unused lately as well. It must be the one Kari Lynn's brother used when he was here, evidenced by the many sports posters on the walls. He couldn't help grinning when he realized they were all athletes of days gone by. A long forgotten baseball bat stood in one corner, a ball and glove nearby. Apparently her brother hadn't been to the cabin in some time.

At the end of the hallway a door stood ajar.

"Lord, please let me find her here asleep," he whispered.

He eased the door open.

"Kari Lynn, are you in here?"

One of the twin beds was rumpled as though someone slept in it recently, but it was empty now. Sunlight flooded across the room from one of the windows and the opened shutters flapped in the breeze. Her purse hung on the back of a chair. A half-eaten box of crackers spilled onto the floor. But there was no sign of her anywhere. No clothes, nothing.

As he stepped around the foot of the bed he held his breath, half expecting to find her crumpled on the floor. A sigh of relief escaped when she wasn't there.

Then where was she? He went back outside and looked in her car, although he wondered why she would be there. But he had to find her.

It was empty.

He walked toward the lake hoping to see her strolling along the beach. There was no sign of anyone. Not even tracks in the damp sand.

When he passed the wooden rowboat turned upside down

beside the dock, he lifted the edge and peeked under, although he didn't expect to find her there. But it didn't hurt to look. Especially if she was trying to hide from him.

His heart thumped against his chest as all kinds of thoughts of what happened to her flew through his mind. If someone saw her come here alone he could only imagine what they might do. He quickened his steps, calling her name as he searched the clearing around the cabin. He even looked in the storage shed filled with equipment for summer time activities.

No Kari Lynn.

Even if she didn't want to see him, he wished she would at least show her face. If for no other reason than to tell him to leave her alone.

"Father," he began to pray, "You know where she is right now. Protect her from harm, Lord. Please help me know where to look that I haven't already checked. Comfort her, wherever she is."

He combed the edge of the forest that bordered the cabin site looking for some clue of where she might be. Maybe some footprints in the soft ground or broken branches, anything to indicate someone had passed by here.

That's when he noticed the barely discernible path between the trees. He decided to follow it, although he couldn't imagine her out here in the woods.

When he reached the shade of the trees a cold wind hit his face and goose bumps rose on his arms. He went back to his car to retrieve his jacket and the one he brought for Kari Lynn.

Once more he started along the path, keeping an eye on the trail for any sign of recent passage. Pine needles and dead leaves made a deep carpet on the ground and it would be difficult to see any footprints here.

"Kari Lynn. Where are you? Don't hide from me, please."

His mind raced with all kinds of things that could happen to her. Maybe she got lost in the dense growth of trees, although he doubted that would happen. She was too familiar with the area. The thought foremost in his mind was that someone accosted her.

Hot tears ran down his face as he walked deeper into the woods, but he kept his eyes and ears tuned to his surroundings.

A rustle in the trees to his left startled him.

"Kari Lynn?"

A rabbit scurried for cover, and his heart sank. He closed his eyes and breathed another prayer for her safety and wisdom in finding her.

He pushed on, his ears alert to any noise or movement in the trees. The only sounds were the sigh of the wind through the pines and an occasional call of a bird or a squirrel's chatter.

Then he heard something else. He stopped to listen. It sounded as though someone was crying. Could it be? Perhaps she was hurt. Or...

Quickening his pace, he kept his ear tuned to the sound ahead of him. After going a short distance he could make out the sound more clearly. It was someone crying. Sobs echoed through the woods ahead of him. He started to run.

chapter 10

"I'm coming," Troy called as he stumbled along the path. Tears blurred his vision, and he had to catch himself once to keep from falling when a root caught his foot. The sound seemed to be close, but he couldn't see anyone. "Where are you, Kari Lynn?"

Although he peered into the trees for a glimpse of her there didn't seem to be anyone there.

Then he realized the crying seemed to come from above him. A ladder he hadn't noticed before climbed the trunk of a large maple tree. He looked up. A tree house was almost hidden among the thick branches.

It didn't take him long to scramble up the ladder and poke his head through the opening in the floor. He waited a moment for his eyes to adjust to the dim light, but then he saw her. She was huddled in the corner of an old arm chair.

"Kari Lynn, are you all right?"

Heaving himself into the room, he rushed to her side. He dropped to his knees and wrapped the jacket he brought around her and pulled her into his arms. When he noticed she was shivering, he lifted her from the chair, dropped into it and settled her on his lap, cradling her head on his shoulder.

"Shh, it's all right, honey. I'm here now."

There was no response. Only heart wrenching sobs that seemed to shake her entire body. She lay limp in his arms as he stroked her hair with his hand.

"It's going to be all right," he whispered.

That's when he realized something might have happened to her and she was hurt, and he held her a little away from him to let his gaze roam over her.

"Are you okay? Are you hurt?"

He thought she shook her head, though he couldn't be certain. He pulled her close again and continued to rock her in his arms.

After several minutes he felt her push slightly away from him and she looked into his face.

"Wh..where did you come from?" she asked between sobs. "I…I didn't think anyone kn…knew where I was. How…how did you get here?"

Tears of relief flowed down his face but he ignored them.

"I'm so glad I found you. You don't know how worried I was. When I couldn't find you I thought something terrible happened to you."

"But…but how did you know I came to…to the cabin?"

"It did take some investigative work. But once I got here and couldn't find you anywhere, I was beside myself. I just knew something bad happened to you."

He let his eyes roam over her again.

"You weren't…No one tried to…"

Again he thought she shook her head.

"But…but how did you know I was up here in the tree… tree house?"

"It did take a while. But then I heard you crying and followed the sound. My heart nearly stopped when I heard that, certain you were lying somewhere injured."

He relished the feel of her as she snuggled back against him.

"I...I must look terrible," she whispered as she attempted to wipe the tears from her face.

"You look wonderful, never more beautiful than you do at this moment. I thought I lost you. When my phone calls were unanswered and you weren't at your apartment when I came by, I almost went out of my mind. I had no idea where you were."

Tears of relief dampened her hair as he kissed the top of her head. "Thank God I found you. I don't know what I would do if anything happened to you."

He pulled her closer into his arms. Although she was no longer sobbing as hard, tears were still flowing down her cheeks.

When he noticed her shiver, he opened his jacket and wrapped it around her. Maybe some of his body heat would warm her.

"When did you come out here? You weren't here all night, were you?"

"No, I stayed in the cabin last night. When it started to get light I came out here."

Neither said anything for several minutes. Still snuggling as deep as she could in his arms, Kari Lynn finally broke the silence.

"I used to spend a lot of time in this old tree house when I was growing up. Our family spent most of our summers at the cabin. We always enjoyed it here with its peace and quiet. I wiled away many hours up here, reading and dreaming about the future."

She swiped at her runny nose with the back of her hand. With the other she reached to the floor and picked up a tattered notebook.

"I couldn't believe my old diary wasn't destroyed by this time. But I found it behind the cushions. Right where I always kept it. I guess no one else knew it was here."

She pulled in a deep breath, allowing the memories to calm her.

"I used to come here and write down all my thoughts and dreams for the future in this book. The tree house was my own special place where I could be by myself, where I could think and dream. My whole life was planned. Everything would be perfect. I would meet a wonderful man, marry him, and raise a beautiful family."

A weak smile managed to break through her tears.

"That was all planned too. We would have four children, two boys and two girls. I thought that made the perfect family."

After a brief glance at Troy she turned away to stare across the room.

"I thought my dreams were starting to come true. I did find a wonderful man and thought we would be married."

Tears came faster now and she tried to hide her face in Troy's jacket.

"But those dreams are all shattered now. I'll never be able to have a family." Sobs shook her shoulders so she could hardly speak. "Not...not even one child!"

It took all her effort, but after several minutes she was able to control her sobs enough to go on.

"That's one of the reasons I came up here, to see if I could find my old diary. I thought if I read some of the things I wrote in it maybe I could make sense of everything going on in my life. But it's so cold I haven't even looked at it yet."

She picked up the book and then snuggled back in Troy's arms. Thumbing through some of the pages, she stopped when she came to one of them. Her eyes moved across the words written on the page, and she brushed at the tears that still ran down her face.

"I wrote this when I just turned eight. My brother and I argued about something and I felt I lost my last friend. My dad came to the tree house and tried to comfort me. He told me I could have a true Friend, One who would never disappoint me the way Dan did. He told me about Jesus and I opened my heart to Him that day."

Although tears were falling so hard she could hardly see, she started to read what she wrote that day.

"Today I asked Jesus to be my best Friend and I know He is. I'm never going to forget Him."

Her shoulders shook and she attempted to stifle her sobs. It was difficult, but she read the rest of the words, brushing away the tears that fell on the page.

"He...He will be my very best friend for the rest of my life. I'll forever do exactly what He wants. His book, the Bible, will be my favorite book from now on and I will re...read it EVERY day. I prom...I promise."

She stared at the page through the tears filling her eyes, unable to force words past them. It took several minutes before she could go on.

"The last time I read those words was shortly before I started college. My parents were ready to move to California and we came to the cabin for a few days relaxation before they left.

"Right after I read this page I remember my dad came to the tree house to tell me we they were ready to leave. I was crying. I hated the fact that they were moving so far away and that I was growing up. I wanted things to stay the same as they always were. I can still hear him say to me, 'You'll make it, just like the rest of us. Remember to keep your eyes on Jesus and everything will be all right. If you forget everything else I tried to teach you, I hope you never forget that important principle. Even though your mother and I may be far away, Jesus is only a prayer away.'"

She looked up at Troy through her tears.

"How did I stray so far from the kind of life I wanted to live? I believed what I wrote that day. They weren't just idle, childish words. I intended to live a life that pleased Him."

"It isn't difficult to see what happened. All we need to do is get our eyes off Him for a little while and it's all downhill from there."

She nodded. "Yes, I know you're right. It's so important for us to stay close to Him. We never know when Satan will try to trip us up."

After leafing through a few more pages, she tucked the book inside her jacket.

"I think I'll take this home with me. It might be good to keep as a reminder."

Both sat immersed in their own thoughts. Neither one spoke. Occasional tears slipped down her face, but for the most part they went unheeded.

She roused when Troy broke the silence.

"So, are you glad you came to the cabin?"

"Yes, I am."

"You don't know how worried I was when I couldn't get in touch with you at home."

"I'm sorry I caused you concern. But things began to crush in on me so hard from all sides I knew I needed to get away. I couldn't abide the four walls of my apartment any longer. I couldn't even stand myself.

"That's when I thought about coming to the cabin. Maybe here in this peaceful place I could think things through. I needed to find some kind of peace in my tormented world. This tree house was always such a solace for me when I was a child and I thought perhaps I could find comfort here again. I needed to do something. I couldn't live with myself anymore the way things were."

"Did you find what you were looking for?"

She nodded.

"I think so. I did a lot of thinking and crying. And praying. For the first time in I don't know how long, I can finally pray and know God hears me. It's horrible when you can't feel His presence. I felt so alone, so forsaken. Everything isn't worked out yet, but at least I know I'm not alone."

Troy's arms tightened around her.

"I'm glad" he whispered. "It hurt to see you so miserable, yet I could do nothing about it."

A shiver shook her body and her teeth chattered.

"Say, you're freezing aren't you? It's too cold out here to be dressed like this. Let's go back to the cabin. I'll build a fire in the fireplace and you'll be warm in no time."

He helped her to her feet and started down the ladder. When she took the hand he offered to assist her down, he couldn't help smiling. It was so good to have her safe beside him again.

When they reached the ground he put his arm around her waist and led her back through the trees.

They had gone just a short distance when he noticed she had begun to lag behind. She seemed to lack the energy to walk the short distance back to the cabin.

"When's the last time you ate?"

She didn't answer.

He stopped and turned her around to face him. The sheepish expression on her face almost made him laugh out loud.

"I guess it was a while ago," she mumbled. "It didn't dawn on me to bring anything with me. The only thing I could think about was getting away from those four walls. I stopped for a hamburger on the way here yesterday morning. Then last night I found a box of crackers in the cupboard someone must have overlooked the last time we were here. I tried to eat some of them, but I couldn't even swallow very many." She made a face and he couldn't miss the way she shuddered. "Yuck. They tasted terrible. They must have been left from years ago they were so stale."

Without thinking, he scooped her in his arms and started to trot down the path toward the cabin. He couldn't help grinning when she began to squirm in his arms.

"What are you doing?" she asked, trying to push away.

"What does it look like? I'm carrying you. I don't want you to collapse from starvation out here in the middle of the forest."

"I can walk. I'm not that weak."

She wriggled in his arms again as though to free herself from his hold, but he held her all the tighter.

"You weren't that strong in the first place, and now you haven't eaten in two days. I'm not about to let you fall in a heap out here."

After settling Kari Lynn on the couch he set about getting a fire started in the fireplace. It wasn't long before a cheerful blaze warmed the room. He noticed a crocheted afghan on the arm of a chair and brought it over, tucking it snug around her.

"Sit here. You'll be warm in no time."

He opened the shutters to let in some of the warm sunshine and then carried in the box of food he brought with him.

Soon steaming bowls of hot vegetable soup, grilled cheese sandwiches, and mugs of hot chocolate were ready. He pulled the table and two chairs close to the roaring fire, then helped Kari Lynn from the couch and settled her in one of them.

It did his heart good to watch her eat. The way she shoveled food in her mouth he was certain she hadn't eaten in weeks. It was a good thing he thought to bring some with him.

"Tired?" he asked when she finished her second mug of hot chocolate. "If you had enough to eat why don't you lie down for a while?"

"I guess I did kind of make a pig of myself, didn't I?" She grinned. "I guess I really was hungry. Thanks for thinking to bring something to eat with you. It never entered my head."

It was good it was to see her smile again. He hadn't seen that in far too long.

"I was glad to see you eat. What little you ate Sunday at the restaurant wasn't enough to keep up your strength. But why don't you take a nap now? You look like you could use some rest."

"I am tired. I suppose all those sleepless nights are taking their toll. I didn't get much here last night either. Too many thoughts running through my mind to let me relax."

He noticed her glance at the dirty dishes as he helped her up from the table.

"Don't worry about them. I'll take care of it."

She looked as though she was going to disagree, but he escorted her down the hall before she could say anything. He nudged her down on the edge of the bed and pulled off her shoes. When she was comfortably settled he pulled warm quilts up to her chin.

"Get some rest now. We'll talk more later."

"Thanks for lunch," she mumbled as her eyes began to close. "And thanks for coming to check on me."

"You just get some much needed sleep now."

After brushing a kiss across her forehead, he returned to the main room to clear the table and wash the few dishes. Now that he found her he could finally relax. He put a few more logs on the fire and sat on the edge of the couch.

His thoughts began to wonder where the future might take them. He knew the only way to keep on the right track was to leave it all with God, the only One who knew what was best for both of them.

"Father, thank You for watching over Kari Lynn and for protecting her from harm," he whispered. "Please keep us both strong while we're here alone in this remote area. Help us keep our eyes on You, our thoughts and actions pure. We don't want to fall into the same trap we were in before. Show us the direction You want us to go from here, whether we are to find a life together or go our separate ways. You know how much I love that girl, Lord, and how difficult it would be for me to give her up. But I know Your way is best, whichever it might be. If it isn't Your will for us to have a future together, then it's up to You to give me the strength to let her go. I can never do it on my own."

chapter 11

Troy woke with a start. Goose bumps covered his arms. A glance at the fireplace told him the fire had burned itself out while he was sleeping. No wonder he was cold. Apparently he slept longer than he thought. Rubbing the sleep from his eyes, he got to his feet. After stirring the coals and piling on more wood, a warm blaze soon burned again and he stood before it warm to himself.

A thought crossed his mind that Kari Lynn might not be warm enough, so he tiptoed down the hall and peeked in her room. She appeared to still be asleep. He gently pulled the covers tighter under her chin, but she didn't even stir.

Grateful she was able to get some much needed rest, he made his way to the kitchen to prepare another meal. The way she ate this noon, he better have something fixed when she awoke.

The food was nearly ready when he heard soft footsteps come down the hall. He turned when she stepped into the room. Her arms were wrapped around herself.

"You're cold." He pulled her into his arms. "I hope you were warm enough. Sorry, the fire went out while I was asleep."

"I was plenty warm. It just feels cool out here when I'm out from under all those quilts you piled on me."

"Did you rest well?"

"I did. I haven't slept that good in a long time." Her hand went to her mouth in an attempt to cover a yawn. "How long was I asleep?"

He glanced at his watch. "About four hours. Feel better?"

"Four hours! I thought I just closed my eyes. How could I sleep that long?"

"You were worn out. The extra rest was good for you."

He kissed her lightly on the forehead and then returned to the stove.

"Hungry? I'm fixing something to eat."

"Now that you mention it, I do feel a little empty."

"Good. If you eat the way you did this noon, I'll have you fattened up in no time."

"Fattened up?" He couldn't help chuckling when she frowned at him. "What makes you think I need to gain weight?"

"Look at you. You've lost way too much these last couple of weeks."

When he saw the sheepish grin covering her face when she pulled out the waistband of her jeans, he couldn't help but laugh out loud.

"I guess they are a little loose, aren't they?" she muttered.

His heart nearly broke when she looked up at him and he saw the apologetic expression on her face.

"Why are you doing this?" she asked. "You came all the way up here to find me and now you're even fixing all my meals." A lopsided grin brightened her face. "I do still know how to cook, you know."

After looking at him a moment she added, "It isn't that I don't appreciate everything, but why are you doing this?"

"Because I love you, that's why. It matters to me what happens to you. Can you understand that?"

"I...I think so. But how can you after the way I treated you? I know I wasn't very kind to you."

He took her face in his hands and gazed into her troubled blue eyes.

"It's like I said, because I love you. And because I know you love me. When it's real it doesn't go away just because there are a few bumps in the road."

She didn't reply. He knew if she was truthful with herself she would have to agree.

"Come and sit down," he said as he took her hand and led her to a chair near the fireplace. "Food will be on the table in no time."

A few minutes later he couldn't keep from smiling. She was shoveling hamburger casserole and green beans into her mouth as fast as she ate at lunch. Later, when he brought out a package of chocolate chip cookies for dessert, she grabbed a handful before he could even set them on the table.

"Umm, these are good," she mumbled around a mouthful. "I haven't had one of these in a long time."

She stuffed one after the other into her mouth, hardly finishing chewing one before she shoved in another. This was not typical Kari Lynn Moore behavior. He was now convinced more than ever she wasn't eating at home.

When the meal was finished, she offered to help clean up, but he declined the offer. He led her to the couch and piled in more wood in the fireplace.

"You just rest. I'll take care of the dishes."

The smile she sent him made his knees week. It took all his self-control to keep from crushing her in his arms and declaring his love, but he knew now was not the time.

After putting the final dish in the cupboard he joined her in front of the fire. With an arm around her shoulders he pulled her close. They sat in silence for some time as the flames leaped above the logs, sparks shooting above them.

After several minutes he turned and looked at her. "Feel like sharing what's on your mind? It might help if you talked about what happened."

He gazed at her a moment, waiting for her reaction. She just continued to stare at the fire.

"It's no hurry. I don't want to rush you. Whenever you're ready."

When he folded one of his hands over one of hers, she eased it away and clasped both of hers tightly in her lap, her gaze locked on the blaze in front of them. Perhaps now wasn't the right time to have brought up the subject. It didn't look as though she wanted to talk about it right now.

It was several minutes before she spoke. She continued to stare at the fire as though the words she wanted to say might somehow be hidden there. After pulling in a deep breath she began in little more than a whisper.

"I think I do want to talk about it. It might be good for me. At least Laura keeps telling me it will help."

She pulled in another deep breath.

"You have no idea how difficult all this is for me. No one can imagine what it's like unless they've been through it."

Troy pulled her closer. He had some idea what it was like, and it wasn't easy for him either. But he said nothing.

"I felt so guilty about what we were doing. I knew it was wrong. I learned long ago what the Bible teaches about that kind of relationship outside of marriage. But once we started I didn't want to turn back, even though I knew we should.

"Then when I found myself pregnant I didn't know what

to do. How could God forgive me for what I was doing? And how could I face our friends once they found out I was such a hypocrite?"

A tear slipped down her cheek but she didn't seem to notice. After a moment's hesitation she turned to look at him.

"When you insisted on the abortion I knew it wasn't the answer to our situation. But you refused to listen to me. I didn't know how you could even consider it."

How many times had he asked himself that same question? He still couldn't believe he ever forced her to do such a thing.

Kari Lynn looked back at the flames snapping and sputtering on the burning logs.

"I almost decided I wasn't going to go through with it, regardless of what you wanted."

He tightened his arm around her shoulders. She looked up at him with an expression that begged him to understand, tears ready to spill from her eyes.

"I was…I was going to kill our baby. What gave me the right to take the life of a little one who never even took its first breath?"

Tears began to roll down her cheeks.

"When it came time to go to the clinic, I thought I couldn't go through with it. All I could think about was what I was going to do to an innocent little child."

Her tears came faster now, but she continued in spite of them.

"When you came to the apartment that morning to take me to the clinic, I was ready to tell you I wasn't going to do it. But you stood there looking at me with such a cold expression on your face I didn't think I had a choice. So I went."

She collapsed against his shoulder as though all strength had left her. Her words bit into his heart. He didn't realize he came across so heartless.

She reached past him to a box on the table beside the couch and pulled out a handful of tissues, attempting to mop up the moisture on her face. But it did little good as the tears fell faster than she could wipe them away.

"Even when I went into the room for them to do the abortion, I knew it wasn't right. It wasn't a solution to our problem. I couldn't even believe I was there. But I was sure you wouldn't take me home until it was over, so I went through with it."

"Oh, Kari Lynn," he whispered, his heart nearly broken. "You don't know how I wish I listened to you when you tried to tell me."

She didn't comment, only nodded and looked back at the fireplace.

"When I got home I couldn't stand it any longer. Not only was I sleeping with you, but now I…I killed our little one."

After pulling in a lung full of air she blew it out slowly.

"That's why I was in the park in the rain when you found me. I couldn't even stay in the apartment with myself. I needed to go somewhere. I didn't care that it was raining and I was freezing. I needed to get away from myself. I just wished I could die. At least then I would be with my baby."

His breath caught in his throat as her words registered.

"I had no idea you felt that way. How could I be so blind? Can you ever forgive me for not taking care of you?"

There was no answer. She stared into the crackling flames for several minutes.

"When I woke up in the hospital I was so afraid. I was all alone, and I didn't know what was happening. It was awful. I never felt so forsaken in my life."

Regret consumed him. How could he be so insensitive? He pulled her closer.

Clasping her hands in her lap she stared at them a minute before continuing.

"After surgery, when I found out what happened to me, I was so angry." She glanced at him a moment. "No, I wasn't angry. I was absolutely furious! The only thing I could think of was that you did this to me. And when you came into my room that morning in the hospital to ask for forgiveness I couldn't even stand the sight of you. What gave you the right to come and beg for mercy when my whole life was ruined? Why did you even show up after you told me you were getting out of my life? After all you did to me. You don't even want to know the horrid things I thought about you."

Anger was evident in her voice even now. She shook her head as though remembering something she would rather forget.

"When I got home things were no better. I continued to dwell on what you did to me. I never stopped to think I was as much to blame as you. I didn't have to go along with what you wanted. But I did, even though I knew it was wrong. I tried to forgive you, but I couldn't. The only thing I could think about was how my life is now ruined because of you."

She paused a moment, took another deep breath, and then continued. "I was upset when you assumed I would go to church with you that day." She looked up at him, a lopsided grin on her face. "You never did ask me if I wanted to go, you know. You just said you'd pick me up the next morning. I knew I wouldn't be able to face all the questions people would ask. But I went because Laura told me I should. She said I would have to face our friends sooner or later, and the longer I waited the more difficult it would become.

"When I got home that afternoon I knew I needed to do something. The pastor's message that morning really struck home. I couldn't seem to get it out of my mind."

Then a smile broke through her tears.

"I did come to peace with myself — and with God — this morning up there in the tree house. I asked Him to forgive me, and I know beyond a doubt He has, even though I'm still sorry for everything that happened. I'm not able to completely forgive myself yet, but I know He will help me do that in time. I know I now can go on. I'm not proud of what I did, but I can never change the past. I can only move forward. And I intend to do that now."

"Does…does this mean you forgive me? I know what I put you through was despicable, in God's eyes as well as yours and my own. But I do wish you could find it in your heart to forgive me."

Her gaze was fastened on the hands folded in her lap and she didn't speak for several minutes. It was apparent she couldn't forgive him. At least not yet.

Several minutes went by. Finally her head lifted and she looked him in the eye.

"Yes, Troy, I forgive you. It's difficult, but I know it's what God expects me to do. I can never do it on my own strength, but with His help I know I can. But you aren't the only one to blame. I made my own choices, so I'm as much at fault as you. Can you forgive me for not standing up for what I believed was right?"

"Of course I can. If God is so merciful He can forgive us when we go astray, the least I can do is do the same for you."

He looked at her a moment.

"So does it mean you're willing to start over again?"

She stared into the fire for several minutes as though unsure how to answer.

"I don't know where I want to go from here. So much has happened, and I'm still somewhat confused. I know I still love you. I don't believe I ever stopped. Even when you came to see me that morning in the hospital I think I still loved you." She lifted her head and grinned. "Although at the time I wasn't about to let you know I did."

Her gaze returned to the blazing logs.

"I was so upset with everything that happened. I thought I needed to put the blame on someone, so it fell on you. I'm sorry."

She looked thoughtful before turning toward him.

"I have missed you. I hated to admit it, even to myself. But I don't know if I'm ready to take up where we left off, where we were before all of this happened. Everything is different now."

"I miss you too. I don't know what to do with myself when you aren't there. Life isn't the same without you. I realize it may be difficult for you to jump back into a relationship like we had before, but I'll give you time. All the time you need."

He looked into the flames shooting upward for several seconds. Finally he turned to her.

"I am curious. Why didn't you answer my phone calls?"

A blush crept up her face.

"I suppose it was rude of me not to talk to you. I heard my phone ring, and I even checked the caller ID. But I didn't want to talk to anyone. It wasn't just you. I didn't even answer my mom's call. Although I was in bed when you called, I wasn't asleep. I'm sorry. Forgive me for not at least letting you know I was okay.

"As soon as it got light yesterday morning I got up, jumped in my car, and drove up here. I don't know what I was thinking when I didn't bring anything with me. I'm not sure I even gave thought about whether I would stay overnight or anything else. The only thing I knew was that I needed to get away from there."

"It's obvious things are now settled in your mind." He tightened his arm around her shoulder and smiled. “In spite of the fact you had me worried to death, I believe coming here was the best medicine you could find. We won’t worry about the future. It will take care of itself. As long as we let God guide us in His way.”

Kari Lynn smiled and snuggled into the arm he wrapped around her.

When she awoke the next morning the weight Kari Lynn carried for so long was gone. Not that everything was over yet. She still wished it never happened, but at least she didn’t feel the load of guilt she carried before. It now rested with the Lord. She was glad she came to the cabin. Where the future was going to take her she didn’t know. But with God guiding her, she felt at peace and would be able to move forward.

Troy was in the kitchen when she came into the main part of the building. He turned when she stepped into the room.

“Morning. You look rested today. Sleep well?”

He brushed a kiss across her cheek and she couldn’t stop a smile from coming. It felt so right.

“I don’t know when was the last time I slept as well as I did last night. It’s surprising what it can do for a person when you take a load off your mind. Not only take it off my mind, but hand it all over to Jesus.”

He held a steaming mug toward her.

“Care for a cup of coffee? Freshly perked.”

“Mmm, this tastes good,” she said as she savored a sip of the hot liquid. “I didn’t know you could make such good coffee.” She grinned at him over the rim of her cup. “Must be the rustic atmosphere.”

"Oh, I don't know about that. I happen to be a pretty good cook, if I do say so myself."

He turned back toward the stove.

"Were you warm enough last night? I got up a couple of times to put more wood on the fire. Your room is further away from the fireplace though, so perhaps it wasn't as warm as mine. There was heavy frost on the ground when I got up."

She couldn't miss the mischievous grin when he added, "But then some people I know like to sleep the day away and don't get to see it."

The heat of a blush crept up her face when he winked at her.

"Why didn't you wake me?"

"You looked so peaceful when I peeked in on you I hated to disturb you. I knew you needed the rest."

Breakfast was soon on the table and they sat down to eat. Her heart fluttered when Troy took her hand in his and bowed his head.

"Father God, there's so much to thank You for this morning. First of all, Kari Lynn is safe. Thank You that You gave her relief from the burden she tried to carry by herself. I'm so thankful You are willing to forgive us whenever we go astray. I ask now that You lead us in our future plans. May we never take our eyes off You the way we did in the past. Thank You for this nourishment and for all Your many blessing to us. Amen."

She savored the last drop of coffee from her mug and set it on the table.

"Want some more?" he asked.

"Yes, please. That was good, very good."

When he rose from his chair and reached for the cup, she let her gaze follow him as he went to the counter and poured more of the steaming beverage into both their mugs. His smile when he set the cups back on the table made her pulse race.

"You're too good to me, Troy Hoffman. I don't deserve the likes of you."

"I'm sorry, but I'm afraid you're mistaken. It's me who doesn't deserve you."

"Want to argue about it?"

"Maybe we deserve each other."

She didn't miss the mischievous gleam in his eye.

His expression changed to one of seriousness as he added, "I just thank God I found you safe and well. You don't know how worried I was when I couldn't find you, both when I went to your apartment and then when I got here. I thought of all kinds of things that could have happened, none of them good. I was nearly beside myself."

"Thanks, Troy. I mean it. For everything. I don't know what I would do without you."

They explored around the cabin the rest of the day. She showed him many of the places she used to play when she was a child and Troy could tell she enjoyed the memories it provided of happier days.

After dinner they decided to stay one more night. It was already almost dark, and rather than drive the winding roads tonight it would be best if they waited until morning.

Troy lay awake in his room for some time as he relived the past two days. Kari Lynn looked so much better than she did on Sunday. He was sure she was well on her way to recovery. The color was back in her face and she appeared to be stronger physically. Even the haunting look he noticed in her eyes ever since the abortion was gone. She looked more like the person he knew and loved again.

Perhaps coming to the cabin was the best thing for her. She seemed pretty much back to herself again, and he knew she was also starting to get things straightened out spiritually. That was the most important area of her life that needed recovery. Something they both needed.

He lay on his back and listened to the soft breathing of the one he loved in the room next door. The wind whispered through the trees and the waves lapped on the shore of the lake. It wasn't long until the peaceful sounds lulled him to sleep.

After breakfast the next morning they packed up their things to go back to the city. He watched as Kari Lynn looked around her, a wistful expression on her face.

"I wish I could stay longer," she said with a loud sigh. "It's so peaceful here. In fact I gave it serious consideration when I woke up this morning. There's no reason for me to go home since I don't go back to work for a couple more weeks."

"You want to stay longer? I told them at the office I wanted to take the rest of the week off. I didn't know what condition I might find you in when I got here, so I wanted plenty of time to give you all the help you needed."

The whispering pines and shimmering lake were indeed an enticement to stay. It took all his willpower to ignore the call.

"It is tempting," he admitted, "and I would like to stay longer myself. It's so quiet and restful here. I see why your dad came here for the summer."

He took Kari Lynn's hand in his and gazed into her eyes a

second or two.

"But I think it would be best if we went back home. With only the two of us here, it would be easy to get caught up in temptation again. There's no way I want to let that happen."

He heard Kari Lynn breath a loud sigh.

"I suppose you're right. Even though I think I learned from past mistakes, there's no need for us to try to find out how strong we are."

chapter 12

Kari Lynn welcomed the idea of going back to work. It was good to be around other people after the lonely days in her apartment. And the work piled on her desk gave her ample excuse to not have to think about what happened.

The cacophony of voices was music to her ears when she walked into the lunchroom. When she didn't see anyone she knew she made her way toward an empty table, nodding at three women engrossed in conversation at the one next to it.

She had just taken the first bite of her sandwich when she overhead one of the women say, "I'm pregnant."

Although she didn't intend to eavesdrop, sitting right next to their table it was unavoidable since they were talking louder than necessary. She tried to ignore the conversation. It wasn't easy to hear other women talk about being pregnant.

"I don't want a baby right now," the woman went on. "Maybe someday, but not at this point in my life. I love this job and I don't want to give it up. I'm not ready for the inconvenience of a child. I think I'm going to take Friday and get rid of it." She looked from one woman to another. "What would you do?"

The words thundered in Kari Lynn's ears. Her stomach

churned as her own recent situation rushed to her mind.

"I wouldn't want the complication of a baby either," a friend replied. "I'd get an abortion if I was in your situation."

Kari Lynn pushed her sandwich aside. The thought of putting another bite of food in her mouth almost gagged her.

"I agree," another one said. "Who needs to be tied down with a baby at this point of our career? And think about your social life. No one will want to ask you out when you have a baby. Yes, I think you're wise to have an abortion. I know I would."

She couldn't believe they were talking about this as if killing a baby was no different than choosing a new hairstyle. Although she knew they didn't intend for her to hear their conversation, she was unable to ignore it. It hit too close to home.

"How far along are you?"

"I'm not sure. I did one of those home pregnancy tests, and I think probably about two months."

Two months! Kari Lynn stared at the woman. *That's how far along I was when I had my abortion.* She clamped her teeth over her lower lip to keep from jumping up and speaking her mind.

"Only two months? Then what are you concerned about. It isn't even a baby yet. It's nothing more than a mass of cells. There wouldn't be any reason not to have an abortion at that stage."

Unable to keep silent any longer, Kari Lynn leaped to her feet and stared at the women at the other table.

"How can you say that? It makes no difference if she's just two months along. She would still be killing a baby if she had an abortion."

The women looked at her in surprise, but no one responded to her outburst. Her insides trembled.

"What do you mean it's nothing but a mass of cells? Don't you know it's already a baby? It isn't fully developed, but it is still a living human being. Its heart has even started to beat. How can you even think about destroying it?"

She could listen no more. If she didn't leave now she knew she would either burst into tears or say something she would later regret. Maybe both. Snatching her uneaten lunch from her table she dashed across the room. The women stared after her, mouths gaping.

The door of the lady's room crashed against the wall when she burst in. The room was empty, much to her relief. Tears she could no longer hold back came before the door even closed behind her. Sobs shook her shoulders as she turned the lock of the nearest stall.

Her lunch break was over, she was sure. But she didn't want to leave the privacy the room offered, afraid of what she might do or say if she met one of the women from the lunchroom. She tried to be a witness for Christ at work, and it would do irreparable damage if she lost her temper and gave them another piece of her mind.

Splashing cold water on her face did little good, but it was time to get back to work. She eased the door open a crack and looked down the hall. No one was in sight. Hopefully she wouldn't meet one of her coworkers on her way back to her desk with her eyes so swollen from crying.

Somehow she managed to make it through the day, although she might just as well have gone home. Her mind refused to stay on her work. The women's words continued to haunt her as she counted the minutes until time to leave the building.

The solitude of her apartment was a welcome relief. As soon

as she arrived home she sank into the cushions of her favorite chair. The ordeal in the lunchroom seemed to have sapped all of her energy, and within minutes she was asleep. But her eyes no sooner closed than visions of tiny babies with outstretched arms began to float behind her lids.

The peacefulness of the apartment was shattered by the ring of her cell phone. Startled, she groped to find it before the caller hung up.

"'Lo," she muttered still half asleep. She rubbed at her eyes in an attempt to erase the images still floating through her mind.

"Did I interrupt a nap?" she heard Troy say. "You sound half asleep."

"I guess I did doze off, but I'm glad you woke me."

"Bad day at work?"

"No more than usual. Why?"

"You sound upset. Something you want to talk about?"

"I'm all right. I guess I'm not quite awake yet. I was tired when I got home and fell asleep."

"Sometimes it helps to talk about what's bothering you. Why don't I stop by on my way home from work and we can discuss it?"

"That's not necessary. I'm okay. Just a little tired is all. I'll probably go to bed early tonight and get some extra rest. I guess I'm still not used to the demands of work."

It wasn't exactly the truth, but she knew it wasn't a good idea for them to spend so much time together. The more they saw of each other the more difficult it would be to drop their relationship. Something that was bound to happen sooner or later. As much as she hated to think about giving him up, she knew it was the right thing to do.

They talked a few more minutes. Before he hung up Troy

told her he would be there in half an hour.

She laid the phone on the end table, then shuffled toward the bedroom to change out of her work clothes.

After slipping into a comfortable pair of jeans and a sweater, she paced the floor waiting for Troy to arrive. Why did he continue to act as though everything was back to the way it was before? It would never work. Not anymore.

It wasn't long before she heard his characteristic knock. As usual, it sent a tingle up her spine in spite of her attempt to overlook it.

"Come on in," she said as she pulled the door open, although she knew her voice lacked its usual enthusiasm.

Troy settled on the couch and patted the seat beside him. She dropped into the corner at the other end and curled her long legs under her, avoiding his gaze. Picking at her sweater, she pretended to remove bits of lint that weren't there.

"Okay, what's bothering you?"

"I told you it was nothing."

He slid across the empty space between them and gently turned her face toward him. She bit the inside of her lip and tried to ignore the thrill of his touch, but with little success.

"Kari Lynn, I know you well enough to know when something is wrong."

He gazed into her eyes until she had to turn away.

"I want to help you, believe me I do. When you hurt, I hurt. Love is like that."

"Please don't say things like that." She nibbled on her left thumb nail a moment. "You know our relationship can never be the same as it was. In fact, I think it would be best if we didn't see each other anymore. It will only be that much more difficult later on when we decide it's best to call off our relationship."

She couldn't miss how his jaw dropped as he stared at her in disbelief. Obviously her suggestion took him by surprise.

"You don't mean that, do you? You know I still love you. I never stopped. How can you even think about something like that?"

No, she didn't want to think about it, but she knew things could not continue the way they once were. It was not a snap decision. She spent agonizing hours mulling over the best course of action and knew this was best for both of them. Now she needed to make him understand there was no longer a future for them. To continue their relationship could only lead to a dead end after everything that happened, so there was no need to prolong the inevitable.

The room echoed with silence as neither one said anything.

After several minutes Troy turned to her.

"Okay, let's not worry about what's ahead right now. What happened at work today? I know something must have. I want to help you."

She pulled in a deep breath and let it out slowly. He always knew when something bothered her and wouldn't give up until she told him. She might just as well get it over with.

"I overheard some women talk at lunch today. They said some very upsetting things."

It was difficult to even think about the conversation, much less talk about it, but he was waiting for her to continue.

"One of the girls said she wanted to get an abortion."

She looked up at him.

"How can people consider something like that? Oh, I know I had one, but we didn't give it enough thought before I did it. I'm sure we would have changed our minds if we just took the time to think and pray about it. This woman said she simply didn't want to be tied down with a baby so why not get rid of it. The other women agreed with her that it was the right thing to do. They talked about it as though it was no big deal. How could they do that?"

She searched Troy's face for an answer.

"One of them even went so far as to say it isn't a baby yet, only a mass of cells. So it wouldn't be wrong to destroy it."

A tear slipped down her cheek when she closed her eyes. Although she tried to ignore the feel of Troy's finger when he touched her cheek to wipe it away, it was impossible. But she couldn't let it get to her. A sudden weariness overcame her and she let herself collapse in the corner of the couch.

"How could they say something like that? How could they even think the tiny baby she's carrying isn't a human being? How, Troy?"

Her shoulders began to shake with uncontrollable sobs.

"I knew I carried a baby the moment I thought I might be pregnant, not that it would one day become one. It was a child the moment it was conceived. How could they be so ignorant of the facts?"

"I'm sorry you had to hear their conversation. But I totally agree with you. I firmly believe the moment a baby is conceived it's a human being. It may not look like one yet at that stage, but it doesn't take long for all the intricate parts to develop."

He picked up her Bible from the table beside the couch and leafed through the pages until he came to the verse he was looking for.

"Here in Psalm 139 God tells us He knew our days before one of them even came to be. He knit us together in the womb. He was there in the very beginning. So how can we believe it isn't a baby? He also tells us He knew us when we were still in our mother's womb."

He turned a few more pages.

"And here in the first chapter of Jeremiah He says even before He formed us He knew us. Yes, a baby starts out as one cell dividing, but there is life in even that one cell. God already breathed life into it. That tells me it isn't just a mass of cells, it's His creation."

Those last words hit her almost as though he struck her. Her hands flew to her mouth.

"His creation! I never thought of it that way before. God created the little one I destroyed, didn't He? And I killed the work of His hands. Right in front of His face!" She ignored the tears streaming down her cheeks and could only stare at Troy. "How could I do such a thing?"

"You're right, we did. I never thought of it that way myself before. But it is a sobering thought."

"What must God think of me? He watched everything that went on in that room. It wasn't something done in secret. He saw it all."

Pages rustled as Troy turned back to the verse in Psalms. When he looked at her again, regret was evident on his face.

"I wish I took the time to see what the Bible said before I insisted you have the abortion. If I'd seen it in this light, I'm sure I would never have considered that option."

His hands closed over hers and he looked deep into her eyes. Neither spoke for several minutes as they pondered this new revelation.

After a couple minutes Troy turned to her.

"I think I understand why the conversation upset you and why it affects you this way. And I'm sure, like you, I'll be upset when I hear someone treat it so lightly. I would give anything to be able to go back and do things over, but, as I said before, there isn't that option."

"No, there isn't."

She pulled her hands from his grasp and twisted her fingers together in her lap.

"I thought I was strong enough to start putting the past behind me. But when I heard those women talk about it today I couldn't help thinking about the little baby I destroyed."

Lifting imploring eyes, she couldn't help ask, "Will I ever be able to forget what I did? Really put it in the past?"

"I wish I knew what to tell you. I know God has forgiven us and I would like to forget it ever happened, but we can't continue to dwell on it. We just have to turn it all over to Him. That's all we can do."

"I suppose you're right. It's just so difficult. When I heard those women treat the subject so casually I wanted to scream." She gave him a self-conscious grin. "I did let them know what I thought about what they were saying, but I don't think they appreciated it."

She stared at her hands as she picked nonexistent fuzz balls from her sweater.

"I suppose it will get better with time. I just wish I was as much at peace with it as you are. I thought things were getting a little better. Those dreams — "

Her hand flew to her mouth and she stopped mid-sentence.

"Dreams? What kind of dreams are you talking about? You never told me about any."

They seldom came anymore, and she hoped he would never need to know about the horrible visions she experienced right after the abortion. But now that she let it slip she would have to tell him.

"When I woke up in the emergency room after the abortion,

these awful visions of tiny babies floated in front of my eyes. They pointed at me and seemed to scream at me as though I did something awful to them. Sometimes they pleaded with me to help them. It was terrifying. At times they accused me of destroying them. I couldn't get away from them."

Troy's arms went around her and she tried to relax as he rocked her gently.

"Oh, honey, I'm so sorry. I wish I could have chased them away for you. How long did this go on?"

"The first few days and nights were horrible. It seemed every time I closed my eyes they were there."

Tears streamed down her face but she ignored them.

"After I laid everything at Jesus' feet in the tree house, they pretty much stopped. But now after the conversation at work I'm afraid they are going to be back. I closed my eyes for a minute when I came home this afternoon, and there they were. Tiny babies accusing me all over again."

"Let's pray they don't come back again," Troy whispered as his hand rubbed across her back. Taking her hand in his, he bowed his head.

"Father, we know these horrid dreams do not come from You. They can only be from the evil one, the one who delights in accusing us. We pray You will take control of the situation and intervene whenever they come to torment her."

"Thank you, Troy. I do appreciate your concern."

His eyes probed hers. "You okay?"

She sighed. "I will be. I just need to get everything back in perspective again."

He nodded but didn't reply. His arms went around her and she cuddled in his embrace. She reveled in the feel of his arms. If only she could stay here forever. But it could never be.

After sitting in silence for several minutes she pulled herself from his arms and curled up in the corner of the couch, the day's events still rushing through her thoughts.

Finally Troy stirred and got to his feet. She heard him say something, but her mind was elsewhere and she didn't hear what he said. Attempting to push her musings aside, she roused and turned to him.

"I'm sorry, what did you say? I'm afraid I wasn't listening."

"I asked if you wanted to go get something to eat. Later we can come back and watch a video or something. Whatever you want to do. We're not going to solve all our problems by sitting here thinking about them. Besides, I think it's about dinner time. How about it?"

She considered his suggestion for a minute. Then she remembered what she told herself earlier about it being best if they didn't continue seeing each other. Her stomach rumbled, although she tried to ignore it. Maybe she could go to dinner with him, but then she needed to tell him it was time for them to go their separate ways.

"I guess I am a little hungry. I don't know about watching a movie though. I think I just want to come home and go to bed early. I'm still not back to my normal self, and today was tiring."

Dinner was quieter than usual. She wasn't as hungry as she thought, and ended up pushing more food around her plate than she put in her mouth. The looks Troy sent her several times didn't go unnoticed, but she was glad he didn't ask her what was wrong. Thoughts whirled through her mind and she found herself close to tears several times when she remembered what she needed to do when he took her home.

"Get some rest if you're tired," he told her when he brought her home from the restaurant. "Maybe we can do something together tomorrow."

Kari Lynn turned away from him. She couldn't look at him so she stared across the room.

"I meant what I said earlier. I don't think we should see each other anymore. Things aren't the same as they used to be. There's no use kidding ourselves into thinking we can have a future together. Not anymore."

His mouth opened to reply, but she held up her hand.

"No, it's best if we go our separate ways now. There's nothing to gain by prolonging it."

She opened the door and motioned for him to go.

"Goodbye, Troy. When you take time to think about it you will realize it's best this way. Please, just leave now."

He looked at her for a minute as though he wasn't going to do as she asked. She thought he might argue with her, but he turned and stepped into the hall, pulling the door closed behind him.

As soon as the door closed she leaned against it and listened to his footsteps go down the hall. It was obvious he still loved her and expected to take up where they were, but she knew she could never do that.

It was so difficult to let him go when she still loved him. Just as much as ever. But she couldn't pretend nothing had changed. It wouldn't be fair to let him believe there was a future for them. She could never marry him. Not now.

With a sigh she moved away from the door.

"I don't want to give him up, Lord. I still love him too much for that. Oh, God, why did this have to happen? I know, instead of looking to You for guidance we tried to run things ourselves. It's our own fault."

She made her way to her bedroom and dropped to her knees beside the bed where she talked to her Savior for some time. Finally she rose to her feet and got ready for bed.

The expression on Troy's face when she told him they shouldn't see each other anymore bothered her more than she thought it would. She loved to hear him tell her he loved her, but it wasn't right. Not anymore.

All the events of the day must have tired her more than she realized. She expected to lie awake for hours trying to forget the conversation at work and the one tonight with Troy. However, she must have fallen asleep almost before her head hit the pillow.

She dreamed she was at work. Troy was there, and women were gathered around him. They all said they were pregnant and asked him what they should do. Without hesitation he told each one to get an abortion. Kari Lynn attempted to tell him it wasn't right, but he just pushed her away.

The sharp ring of her phone jolted her back to consciousness. She scrubbed her hand across her face trying to obliterate the dream from her mind.

As she groped through the darkness to grab the phone she knocked it to the floor. After two attempts she finally had it in her hand.

Lord, don't let it be Troy.

"Lo?"

"Oh, were you asleep? I'm sorry. I suppose it is a little late to call."

When she realized it was her best friend, Anne, she pulled herself to a sitting position. She hadn't talked to her for so long she almost didn't recognize her voice.

"I guess I was asleep. But that's okay. I was having kind of an upsetting dream so I'm glad you woke me."

She attempted to stifle a yawn. "So, how are things with you?"

"Everything is fine, but I've missed you lately. How are you? I'm sorry to hear you weren't feeling well. Are you better now?"

"Yes, I am. And thanks for asking. I went back to work again this week."

Guilt tugged at her heart. The two of them used to spend a lot of time together, and she did miss her friend's companionship. But it would be difficult to be with her now. Sooner or later she wouldn't be able to avoid telling her everything that happened.

Anne's voice interrupted her thoughts. "We haven't seen each other in a long time. How about going out for breakfast tomorrow? You know we used to do that a lot on Saturday mornings. I miss the long talks we used to have. Want to meet me at The Grill, say around eight?"

"That might be fun. We haven't talked in a long time, have we? It would be good to do something besides go to work for a change. I don't do much but lie around the apartment since the surgery — "

She drew in a sharp breath, and her hand flew to her mouth as though that could erase her words.

"Surgery? Why didn't you let me know? You mean I missed a chance to help my best friend? I know the first few days after an operation can be rough, especially when you're alone. What kind of surgery did you have? Nothing serious, I hope."

"I don't want to go into it over the phone. Maybe we can

talk about it over breakfast."

"All right. It will be fun to get together again. Just like old times. I've missed some of the things we used to do."

"So have I. Well, see you tomorrow then."

She looked forward to seeing Anne again. Although she hated the idea of anyone knowing what she did, she knew sharing it with someone might help bring relief to the pain she carried. It would be difficult, but she knew her friend would keep a confidence.

Anne was waiting for her at one of the tables when Kari Lynn walked into The Grill the next morning. Tears came to her eyes as the short, dark haired women rushed toward her, her brown eyes sparkling in recognition, her arms wide open. Dashing toward her, she nearly fell into the welcoming embrace.

She had to admit, she had missed her friend these last months, regretting she ever let things come between them. The two women were as different from each other as night and day; Anne as short and dark as Kari Lynn was tall and blond. In their younger years they had often dressed alike, and one time someone addressed them as "Mutt and Jeff, the Bobbsy Twins". They were the best of friends for years, sharing each other's joys and heartbreaks.

They settled at the table Anne had vacated earlier. Like in times past, both women began talking at once, attempting to make up for lost time.

"You didn't tell me what kind of surgery you had," Anne said once they gave the waitress their orders. "I hope it wasn't anything too bad."

The time had come to tell all. Kari Lynn's breath caught in her throat, but she managed to pull in a lung full of air as she looked across the table.

"I hope you won't think less of me as a friend once you find out what I did."

Her friend said nothing, so she plunged ahead.

"A few months ago Troy and I let our relationship go too far and we began sleeping together."

She looked across the table, expecting to see a look of scorn. But there was no indication her news was anything out of the ordinary.

"As you might suspect, I got pregnant. When I told Troy, he didn't take the news very well. In fact he insisted I have an abortion."

Anne still didn't say a word, and her expression gave no clue what she was thinking. Kari Lynn couldn't help wonder what was going through her mind.

"Soon after I got home from the abortion I went for a walk, and I ended up passing out in that little park down the street from my apartment. Troy found me crumpled on one of the benches and called an ambulance to get me to the hospital. When they found out I had the abortion that morning, they rushed me to surgery. Unfortunately, they had to do a hysterectomy because of a big tear they couldn't repair. Compliments of the abortion," she added with a hint of contempt.

She was afraid to look up. Maybe she should leave now. Anne would want nothing to do with her after hearing this.

"Oh, Kari Lynn, I'm so sorry. It must be hard on you. I know you and Troy wanted to have children someday."

Tears clouded her vision.

"We won't be getting married. In fact we're not seeing each

other anymore."

A look of surprise came over Anne's face as she put a hand over hers.

"I'm so sorry. I expected to hear of wedding plans soon. Are you sure everything is over between you?"

"You know how much Troy loves kids." She sniffed back tears and picked at a loose thread on the tablecloth. "I can never marry him now, not when I know I can never give him children."

"Do you still love him?"

The tears she tried to hold back came now, tumbling down her cheeks.

"That's what makes this all so difficult. I do still love him. But I know he would never be happy when we didn't have children. I told him last night everything is over between us. It's best to get it over with now. It would happen sooner or later anyway, so why prolong the agony."

"Things might still work out." Anne patted her hand. "I don't see Troy letting you walk out on him without a fight. Not as much as he loves you."

Kari Lynn nodded, but didn't reply. That might be what her friend thought, but she knew better. It would never work.

The waitress brought their breakfast and their attentions turned to the meal in front of them.

chapter 13

Kari Lynn was surprised to hear her mother's voice on the phone one evening just after Thanksgiving. Guilt tugged at her when she realized she hadn't talked to her parents since the abortion. She kept putting off calling because she was afraid they would ask questions she didn't know how to answer.

"Your dad and I wondered if you could come out for a visit over Christmas," Mrs. Moore said. "We've hardly seen you since you graduated three years ago. We miss you."

She nibbled on the end of her thumb. As much as she would love to visit, she knew she would be unable to avoid telling her parents what she did. She hesitated a few seconds before responding.

"Umm, I don't know Mom. It isn't the best time to travel. I don't know if I could even get a ticket over the holidays."

"Don't worry about that. I was online this morning and they have a good special going on right now. Your brother and his family are coming from Kansas City and I'm getting tickets for everyone. Do you suppose Troy could come?"

"I don't know what he's doing for the holidays, but I'm sure he'll go to Wisconsin to spend time with his parents."

"We would love to have him, but I suppose he does have obligations to his own family. We look forward to seeing you, though. The whole family hasn't spent Christmas together in a long while."

"No we haven't. Not since Dan and Pam were married, if I remember right. That's what, six years ago?"

"You have plenty of vacation time you can take, don't you?"

"Not that much. I used most of it for this year, but I do have a couple personal days I can take. With Christmas on Tuesday, I could make it if I leave Saturday morning."

Mrs. Moore hesitated a minute.

"So how are things with you and Troy? I understand you had some problems a few weeks back."

"We're okay."

She knew that wasn't what her mother was asking, but she didn't know how else to answer.

"We were surprised when he called after you told us you were going to the cabin. He indicated the two of you had some difficulties in your relationship, although he didn't elaborate. So, have you resolved things?"

"We'll be all right."

Kari Lynn pulled in a deep breath. She loved her mom, but she knew her well enough to know there would be all kinds of questions if she even suspected a problem. Perhaps she should tell her parents they were no longer seeing each other, but it was difficult to even talk about it. She knew they would want to know why.

"Well, I hear your dad calling, so I better go. We look forward to seeing you again. I'll email you the information on how to get your ticket."

"I'll be looking for it. It will be fun with all of us together again."

"I'll talk to you later, then."

"Bye, Mom. Thanks for the invitation. And for the ticket."

The moment she laid her phone on the end table she collapsed in her chair. She breathed a sigh of relief that she was able to get by without having to divulge any information. At least not yet. It almost made her not want to visit her parents, as much as she loved them. It would be impossible to spend any time with them without being forced to tell what she did. It would break their hearts when they found out. And she didn't know how she could be around her married brother and his two children. They would be just one more reminder of the family she would never have.

Kari Lynn dozed as the plane flew above the clouds toward California. Her excitement at seeing her family kept her awake most of the night. That, and worrying about how she would answer all the questions she knew were forthcoming.

The pilot's voice over the intercom jerked her awake.

"Ladies and gentlemen, this is your captain. We're approaching Bakersfield Airport and will be landing soon. Please fasten your seat belts. The temperature at the airport is a beautiful sixty-five degrees. I hope you enjoyed your flight and have a great visit here in sunny California. Merry Christmas."

She could hardly wait for people to collect their luggage and make their way down the aisle. It seemed they were purposely moving as slow as they could.

When she finally arrived at the baggage claim, she was surprised to see not only her parents, but her brother, Dan, and his family as well.

Unable to help herself, a shriek of excitement erupted when she saw everyone. She couldn't help dancing in delight as she hugged everyone.

"Why are you all here? I didn't expect anyone but Dad to pick me up."

"Dan's plane arrived just an hour ago so we decided to wait here until you arrived," her dad explained. "It'll be a tight squeeze to fit everyone in the van, but we'll manage," he added with a chuckle.

"So," Dan said as he grabbed her left hand. "I thought you might bring Troy along so we could get acquainted. But I don't see a ring. Don't tell me he has second thoughts about marrying you."

"No, I didn't bring him." She attempted a grin as she added, "It's a good thing he didn't come. We never would fit all of us plus everyone's luggage in the van if there was another person."

Although she had visited her parents in California before, it was still somewhat of a shock when they drove up to the house. With all the family together it seemed as though they should be coming to the old familiar home in Minneapolis.

As she came around the corner she noticed the large wreath on the front door. She smothered a chuckle when she realized it was the same one that decorated their house in Minneapolis for so many years. The red balls tucked among the boughs were beginning to lose some of their shiny paint and the bow at the top was a little droopy. But it still looked like Christmas. Leave it to her frugal mom to never get rid of anything that could still be used.

She followed her brother into the living room and stopped. Her hand flew to her mouth in surprise.

Furniture had been rearranged, making the room somewhat crowded, to make space for the gigantic Norway pine that stood in the corner of the room next to the picture window. The pine scent emitted from the tree drew her toward it.

"Someone's been busy." She turned to her dad. "How many hours did you spend putting on all those lights and decorations? It's beautiful. I can't wait to see it all lit up."

"It isn't Christmas without a tree for the gifts," he replied with a pleased smile.

That's when she noticed the pile of brightly wrapped packages under it.

"It looks like someone else has been busy," she said as she put an arm around her mother.

A wave of homesickness came over her. The room was different, but most of the things in it were the ones she grew up with in Minnesota — the floral couch and her dad's rather worn, but comfortable, recliner. But they didn't look the same in this unfamiliar house.

When she walked into the room where she would stay it felt strange. The full-sized bed she slept in most of her life, covered with the same patchwork quilt, looked different in the strange surroundings. Even the pile of multicolored throw pillows, with the last doll she received for Christmas nestled among them, didn't make the room feel like home. She sank into the rose colored arm chair where she used to spend hours reading her favorite books. It didn't even feel the same.

As she unpacked a few of her things she realized nothing was the way it used to be anymore. This was no longer the home she grew up in and loved. Even her life was changed now.

With a sigh she turned toward the door to join her family down stairs. It was good to all be together again.

Some things never changed, however. Dan pestered her with his jokes and smart remarks the same as usual. She doubted he would he ever grow up.

"What is that wife of yours feeding you?" she asked him that evening when the two of them found themselves alone in the kitchen. "You've put on some weight, haven't you?" She grinned, poking her stocky, dark-haired, brown-eyed brother in the ribs and tugged on the beard he just started to grow. Brother and sister were complete opposites in looks — and temperament. Where she favored their dad in appearance, Dan looked more like their mother, only almost a foot taller than her five-foot-three.

"Guess married life agrees with me." He locked her in one of his usual strangle holds. "Ought to try it yourself. It's good for you."

She shoved him aside without replying. There was no way he would understand what happened, and it was just as well he didn't know.

Before long everyone made their way toward bed. She was ready to head upstairs herself when she decided to get a drink of water first.

Just as she reached in the cupboard for a glass, her dad came in the room from checking the doors for the night.

"Hungry?" he asked. "I noticed you didn't eat much for dinner." He headed toward the refrigerator. "I'm sure we can find something in here to snack on before going to bed."

"No, Dad, I'm not hungry. I just wanted a drink before going up."

She felt him watch her as she set the glass in the sink. This man was always able to see right through her and know when there was something on her mind. Certainly he wouldn't ask questions she wasn't able to answer right now.

"Something troubling you, Kari Lynn? You don't seem yourself tonight."

"No, nothing I can't handle."

"You know I'm always here to listen if you want to talk."

He pulled out a chair for her at the familiar oval, oak table, slightly scarred from years of use.

Slowly she crossed the room and sank into the matching kitchen chair. She would like to tell him everything, but she just couldn't disappoint him the way she knew he would be if he knew.

"How about a cup of hot chocolate while we talk?"

"Sounds good."

He took two mugs from the cup tree and started to prepare the drink. How often in the past had she poured out her troubles to him over these same mugs, at this same table, only in the familiar home in Minneapolis? This simple act of kindness was just one more reminder of how much she loved him. Before she could stop them, silent tears were pouring down her cheeks.

Moments later he set steaming cups of one of her favorite beverages on the table and then settled in the chair next to her. He gently removed the hand she had wrapped around her mug and held in both of his.

"Why don't you tell your old dad what's bothering you," he said in that soft, compassionate voice she remembered so well.

"I don't know if I can, Daddy. You will be so disappointed."

Barely able to see through her tears, she rubbed a sticky spot on the table someone must have missed when they cleaned up after dinner.

"I'm sure it can't be all that bad. Remember you are my daughter, and whatever it is, you know my love for you will always remain. Just the same as always."

"I don't know how you can, not after you hear what I did."

The tears came faster now.

"Oh, Daddy, I love you so much. But if you want nothing more to do with me when I tell you what I did, I'll understand. I don't deserve to be your daughter."

Sobs shook her shoulders as she collapsed in her father's loving embrace.

"There, there, sweetheart. Why don't you tell me what has you so upset and then let me be the judge? Not that I could ever love you any less than I have ever since the day you were born."

Between sobs and wiping away tears she managed to tell the whole story.

"I'm so sorry, Daddy. I don't know why I ever did it. I don't know why we didn't take time to think it over and pray about it. We never really discussed it. He just insisted I have it done right away as though someone might find out if I didn't. Anyway, he went to the clinic the next day and set up the appointment. The following day it was done. I still don't know why I didn't refuse to go through with it. I could have had the baby and raised it by myself, but I just didn't think about it at the time."

His arms pulled her closer and she buried her head in the strong shoulder.

"It's over now, and we can never undo what we did. I'm sorry, Daddy. I wish I could go back and relive those days. But I can't. What's done is done and I can never change it."

Just being in those familiar arms began to soothe her upset soul, reminding her of other times in the past when she shared her problems with him.

"We all make mistakes at one time or other, do things we later regret," he said softly. "I have, your mother has, everyone has. But we can't let it get us down the rest of our lives. Have you asked God to forgive you?"

All she could do was nod.

"Then as far as God is concerned, it's done and over with. Remember the verse in Psalms where He tells us He has put our transgressions away as far as the east is from the west? Then in Isaiah He says He remembers them no more. So if God doesn't hold these things against us, shouldn't we put them away also?"

"But what I did was so horrible. How could He not hold that against me?"

"God isn't like us, He doesn't hold grudges. To Him sin is sin. He doesn't see our sins as big ones or little ones, they are all the same. Yes, we grieve Him when we do things that displease Him, but He's just as grieved when we tell a lie as when we do something we consider big. What He wants is our repentance, regardless of how big or small we think the transgression might be. If you did that, if you asked for His forgiveness, then you can go on. Don't let it continue to get you down."

"But I feel so horrible about what I did. I can't just forget it."

"No, I'm sorry to say we never get over regretting what we did, but we must rest in the fact that God has forgiven us and not try to hang on to it. We are human beings, and we will do things that displease Him. We still have temptations. But if we stay close to Him we will be less likely to do things that grieve Him."

Neither spoke for several minutes. She started to relax in the love radiating from her dad's presence.

"Why didn't you let us know?" he whispered. "You know your mom and I are always here for you."

"I couldn't. I didn't want you to know what I did. I know I disappointed you. You and Mom taught me better than that. I'm sorry. I still don't know why I had the abortion. I wish I never listened to Troy when he insisted it was the only thing to do."

"It's over now. Don't keep reliving the past. Just remember to look to God for wisdom the next time temptation comes your way."

When he started to gently wipe the tears from her face they almost started all over again. His demonstration of love and compassion was more than she deserved, but this was why she loved him so much. He always seemed to understand and make things better.

"Why don't you go up to bed and get some rest?" He kissed the top of her head. "Tomorrow is a new day. Don't let your past ruin it for you."

"Alright, Daddy."

She stood, then leaned over and placed a kiss on his cheek. "Thank you for being so understanding."

The next couple days she attempted to enjoy her family, but Dan's constant teasing about when she was going to settle down to married life soon became old. When it got to be too much she went off to her room by herself. If anyone noticed, no one mentioned it.

Christmas morning was especially difficult. She was quiet as the family opened their gifts. Everyone's attention was focused on the excited children as they ripped open the packages piled beside them and she hoped no one realized she wasn't involved in the excitement.

When all the gifts were open, six-year-old Stephanie brought her new doll to her aunt.

"Would you play with me and my dolly, Aunt Kari Lynn?"

Tears clogged her throat as she looked at her little blond, blue-eyed niece, so much like pictures she recalled seeing of herself at that age. But the sight of her also reminded her of a little girl of her own she would never have.

"Not right now, honey."

Disappointment clouded the girl's face as she shuffled to the rocker and began to cuddle her doll.

She felt everyone look at her, questions obviously on their minds, but no one commented. Pulling in a deep breath, she walked from the room. Just the thought of playing with her niece and nephew was another reminder of Troy and how much he loved children. She knew if he was here he would be on the floor playing with both Tyler and Steph. It was all she could do to control her tears until she reached her room.

In some ways, the few days the family spent together flew past. It was good to all be together again. Yet the time seemed to drag. Stephanie and Tyler hung on her constantly, begging for her attention. She loved them and wanted to play with them, but she just couldn't. It hurt too much.

As difficult as it was to be around the children, she hated saying goodbye to Dan's family as they left to go back to Kansas City the day after Christmas. The house now echoed with emptiness with the boisterous children — and her constantly annoying brother — gone. She wandered from room to room, not knowing what to do with herself. She noticed her mother look at her several times as though she wanted to say something, but she never did.

That evening she was in her room packing for her trip home

the next day. Her mother stopped in the doorway, studying her for a minute. Then she came in the room and sat on the bed beside the half-packed suitcase.

"Your father told me last night what happened. This is eating away at you, isn't it? I noticed you didn't seem yourself."

All Kari Lynn could do was nod.

"You still love him, don't you?"

"Yes I do. That's what makes all of this so difficult. I would love to marry him, but I can never punish him this way. He would never be happy."

Tears blurred her vision as she looked at her mother, begging her to understand.

"Mom, you know I can never have children now. And he adores them. That's why it was so difficult for me to be around Dan's kids when they were here. They reminded me so much of Troy and all the attention he always showers on kids. If he had come with me, I know he would've been down on the floor playing with them."

She picked up a tissue from the nightstand to blow her nose and then sat beside her mother.

"I told him the last time I saw him we shouldn't see each other anymore. There was no need to continue as though there could be something for us in the future." She buried her face in her mother's shoulder. "We needed to go our separate ways sooner or later, so no use to prolong it. Why make it any more difficult than it was?"

"Does he love you?"

"I guess he does. At least he told me he does. I haven't talked to him since I told him we shouldn't see each other anymore. Oh, Mom, I don't deserve someone like him. He treated me with such love and consideration, even when I was so horrid to him."

"Do you think there is any way the two of you can get back together? I hate to see you go your separate ways. He's a good man. And he is part of the whole problem, you know. It's his fault as much as yours you can't have children. He would never have a reason to hold that against you."

"It sounds easy, but I know he would always be unhappy with no little ones. No, Mom, as difficult as it is, I think it's best this way. I love him too much to ever do something like that to him."

"I'm sure things will work out in due time. Pray about it and I know God will show you His will. Your dad and I will pray too, but the most important thing is that you know you are in God's will."

Kari Lynn felt her mother looking at her.

"Is this why you went to the cabin that day? We thought it seemed rather strange."

"I had to get away. I couldn't stand it inside those four walls with myself anymore. I'm so sorry. I would give anything if none of it ever happened. I'm sorry I let you and Dad down."

"It is disappointing, I will admit that, but it isn't the end of the world. Go on from here. Don't let your past get you down. Just remember to keep your eyes on Jesus."

"Thanks, Mom. Thanks for being so understanding."

Kari Lynn sniffed back the tears that insisted on coming when it was time say goodbye to her parents and board the plane for the flight home. Mr. Moore took his daughter in his arms, holding her close the way he used to when she was a little girl.

"Take care of yourself, Kitten. Don't be a stranger. Come out anytime you can. Give us a call once in a while to let us know how things are going. We miss those calls you used to send our way. Remember you're always in our prayers."

The use of her dad's childhood nickname for her was almost her undoing. She knew she disappointed him. But by calling her Kitten, she knew he still loved her in spite of all that happened. He expected more than she gave him, yet it hadn't forced him to stop loving her. The tears refused to stop coming. What did she ever do to deserve such loving and understanding parents?

chapter 14

Kari Lynn's cell phone rang as she was coming down the hall. It was in her purse and difficult to get at with her hands full. Fumbling with one hand until she found it, she almost dropped both her purse and the phone along with her keys, on the floor in her haste. She managed to unlock the door and kick it open, tossing her purse and bags of groceries on the breakfast bar. But the caller had hung up by the time she was able to answer. Checking her missed calls, she saw it was her friend Anne, so she called her back.

"Hello."

"Hi, Anne. What's up?"

"Did I call at a bad time? You sound out of breath."

"No, it's all right. I just came from the store. My hands were full of groceries and the phone was in my purse. I was running to get the door open and get rid of everything. Sorry it took me so long."

She dropped into her favorite chair to catch her breath.

"I guess I'm more out of shape than I realized."

She rested a moment until her breathing was back to normal.

"So, what's new with you these days?"

"We finally set the date for our wedding! We talked about

it when we were at Chad's folks over Christmas and decided on February the fourteenth. I always dreamed of a wedding on Valentine's Day, and that turned out perfect this year. Will that work for you? I expect you to be my maid of honor you know. We promised long ago to stand up for each other. I hope you haven't changed your mind."

"Of course not. I'll put it on my calendar right away."

She walked to her desk to make the notation in her planner.

"A Valentine wedding sounds romantic." She glanced at the book in her hand. "February fourteenth. That doesn't give you a lot of time, does it? It's already the second of January."

"No, but it works out perfect this year since it falls on Saturday. And we didn't want to wait another year. Since we don't plan on an elaborate affair it shouldn't take long to put everything together."

After a moment's hesitation, she went on. "Chad wants Troy to be his best man. Will that be a problem for either of you being together in our wedding?"

Kari Lynn didn't know how to answer for a minute.

"N…no," she replied, forcing her voice to cooperate.

It would be difficult, at least for herself. But she couldn't spoil Anne and Chad's wedding just because there wasn't one in the picture for her.

"Don't worry about me," she was finally able to reply. "I can't expect the whole world to be put on hold just because things between Troy and I didn't turn out the way I wanted. I can't let something like that stand in the way of your happiness. I'll be glad to be your maid of honor."

❁❁❁

The following weeks passed in a flurry of activity. The bride had no family nearby so she asked Kari Lynn to help with all the wedding plans. She was soon caught up in Anne's excitement as they pored over the details.

Many times she found herself close to tears as the big day drew near. Any time she was by herself her thoughts turned to her own bleak future and she was unable to keep the tears from coming. If only she could go back to the happier days when she and Troy still looked forward to a wonderful life together. But she couldn't let that dampen her friend's happiness.

The nearer Anne's wedding came, the more often she found herself collapsing in tears when she was alone. She hoped she wouldn't embarrass herself — and the bridal couple — by allowing them to fall during the ceremony.

Several times while they were dressing for the wedding, she was forced to close her eyes and take a deep breath. It took all the effort she could muster to keep her tears under control. The glow of happiness on the bride's face was almost more than she could handle. She tried to suppress her feelings of envy and push her own disappointment aside, but with little success.

Before she was ready for it, the strains of the wedding march reached her ears. She took a deep breath and started down the aisle behind the bridesmaid. Her gaze remained focused straight ahead to avoid even the slightest glimpse of Troy where he stood at the front of the church beside Chad. If she saw him look at her, she knew it would be her complete undoing. Until the rehearsal last night, she hadn't seen him in the last few months.

It was time for Chad and Anne to repeat their vows. She wished she could put her hands over her ears so she couldn't hear. If only she could say those words to Troy one day. It took all the control she could muster to keep from bursting into tears.

The organist began to play the recessional and she wondered how she was going to walk back up the aisle with Troy. It wasn't so bad last night at rehearsal; she just walked beside him without touching him. But this was different. There was no way she could avoid contact today.

He held out his arm and she placed a trembling hand in the crook of his elbow, barely touching his sleeve. Although she felt his gaze on her, she didn't dare glance in his direction. The tears would fall full force, she was sure, if she caught a glimpse of his face. Even without looking, she knew he wore that fabulous smile of his.

After the reception she followed the rest of the people outside to say good-bye to the happy couple. When they climbed into their car without the bride throwing her bouquet, she breathed a sigh of relief. If Anne had thrown them, she knew the flowers would fly straight in her direction. And that was something she didn't need.

Now that everything was over a sudden weariness overtook her. She wished she could go home, but she didn't have a way, and it appeared no one else was ready to leave yet. She collapsed on a chair in the corner and closed her eyes, hoping to catch her breath for a moment.

Troy's voice close to her ear startled her.

"You look worn out. Do you need a ride home?"

This was the last thing she wanted, but she didn't have much choice.

"I hate to ask, but since I came to the church with Anne I don't have my car. And it doesn't appear anyone else is ready to leave. All the help I gave her these last few weeks is starting to take its toll. Now that everything is over I'm about ready to collapse."

The smile he sent her was almost her undoing.

"Of course I'll take you home. I'm sure this was a long day for you. We'll say goodbye to some of the others and then be on our way. After all, everything is over now that the bride and groom are gone."

When they reached her apartment building he accompanied her to her door.

"You look tired. Why don't you go in and get some sleep? I know you worked hard with Anne to take care of all the details."

He took her hand in his before turning to leave.

"Goodnight, Kari Lynn."

The moment the door closed behind him the dam broke. Tears she had somehow managed to hold back all evening began to stream down her face, but she made no attempt to stop them. It was obvious Troy still loved her. It made her angry. She wanted to scream at God for letting all those things happen to her, but she knew it wasn't His fault. She could blame no one but herself.

Invitations arrived in the mail for several more of her friend's weddings over the summer, but there was no way she could attend them. They were just more reminders there would be none in her future. If she did go, she would have to explain why she and Troy were no longer a couple.

The days and weeks crept by. Life was lonelier than she ever experienced before. She stopped attending Calvary Baptist Church ever since that one Sunday she went with Troy because she couldn't face everyone and all their questions. Now there was no one to talk to, no one to go places and do things with.

She still had her work, and Laura came by occasionally. But it wasn't the same.

Although she tried to convince herself she did the right thing by breaking off her relationship with Troy, it wasn't as easy as she hoped to forget the man she hoped to one day to marry. She was still haunted by doubts every day.

She did still keep in contact with Anne. Once she told her friend everything she was comfortable with her. Although now that Anne and Chad were married, they didn't do things together as often. And when they were together, she was reminded of the many times she and Troy did things with Anne and her then fiancé, Chad. The two of them did meet occasionally at The Grill for Saturday breakfast and she always looked forward to those times.

"So, how are things really going for you?" Anne asked one Saturday as they waited for the waitress to bring their meal. "I know you try to put on a brave front, but what's going on inside?"

Kari Lynn was taken aback by the blunt question.

"It's hard, Anne. I never thought it would be this difficult. It seems every time I turn around something reminds me of Troy or something we did together. I watched a movie on TV the other night that we'd watched some time ago. Would you believe, I cried through the whole thing?" She chuckled. "And it was a comedy! But all I could think about was snuggling in Troy's arms while we watched. Then the other day I was driving to work and one of our favorite songs came on the radio. It was all I could do to keep from bursting into tears. Do you think I'll ever get over him?"

"I don't know."

A thoughtful expression came over Anne's face.

"Sometimes I wonder if you did the right thing. Are you

positive this is God's will for you? Maybe it's just what you think is best because of all your pain. Chad and Troy have had some good talks and I know this breakup is very hard on him. Chad says the poor guy gets tears in his eyes whenever he talks about you. He loves you, Kari Lynn. He knows he's hurt you beyond belief, but he doesn't want to lose you."

"I know." Kari Lynn smiled across the table in spite of the tears ready to slip from her eyes. "I've shed buckets of tears thinking about him. But because I love him so much, that's the reason I can't marry him. I want him to be happy, to have everything he wants out of marriage. And that includes children. I would marry him in a heartbeat if I could give him that one thing."

She squirmed under Anne's direct stare.

"Have you considered what Troy wants? After all, he is as much a part of what happened as you are. Don't shut him out. He wants to go on from here."

"You make it sound easy, but it's just not that simple. I can't expect you or anyone else to understand. It's a choice I have to make. Out of love for him."

"Life does go on. Even after tragedy strikes. The only thing we can do is turn it all over to God. He will provide the comfort we need and lead us in the right direction."

"I try to do that, but I'm still frustrated. I often ask myself if I did the right thing by letting our relationship go by the wayside. If we did marry, could we be happy? That question goes through my mind more often than I want." She toyed with a wrinkle on the tablecloth. "Would Troy be satisfied if we didn't have children? Or would he always hold it against me? I couldn't live with myself knowing he didn't have all he wanted from our marriage."

She pulled in a deep breath.

"I've mulled over those same questions so many times, but I still haven't come up with an answer. I try to tell myself it might work, but then the doubts seem to outweigh the positive."

A tear trickled down her cheek and she brushed it away.

"Sometimes I think God wants us to be together. Other times I feel it isn't what He wants for us. Perhaps He made all these things happen for a reason, so that we don't step into something that isn't His will."

A shocked expression came over Anne's face.

"You know He doesn't work that way. Yes, sometimes He lets tragedy come into our lives to teach us some lesson or strengthen our faith. But I don't believe He deliberately does things that will cause us pain."

Kari Lynn bowed her head in thought for a moment as she mulled over her friend's words.

"No, I suppose you're right."

She lifted her head and looked at Anne.

"But how long will this go on? I can't seem to get interested in anything anymore. I'm afraid to go any of the places I used to go, afraid I might run into Troy. I know that sounds silly. The chances of seeing him in a city the size of Minneapolis would be next to nothing. Although I thought I did see him the other day. He and another guy were walking down the sidewalk on the other side of the street. They were busy talking so I don't think he saw me. If it was even him."

Her pulse quickened even thinking about the incident.

"We miss you at church, Kari Lynn," Anne said after a lull in the conversation. "Everyone asks about you and wants to know if you're going to be back."

"I couldn't continue to go there. There's no way I can face any of our friends, although I'm sure they all know what we did by now. It's enough that you know, without everyone else hearing about it. I know you wouldn't say anything. At least I hope not."

She glanced at her friend.

"You haven't, have you?"

"Of course not. We've kept each other's confidences all these many years. I'm not about to start spreading things now."

"I was sure you wouldn't. It's just that I would be embarrassed to death if everyone found out. By the way, does…does Troy still go to Calvary?"

"He didn't come to our Sunday school class at first, but I did see him sometimes in the worship service. He's started to become involved in the group again, although he isn't the same. He just isn't the same easygoing and cheerful guy he used to be."

Anne looked at Kari Lynn a moment.

"This is hard on him too you know."

"That's another reason I can't go there anymore. There's no way I could face him every Sunday."

"Are you attending anywhere? I hope you're not neglecting fellowship with other believers just because of what happened."

"I'm going to Hennepin Avenue Community Church. Laura Brownlee — she's the woman I told you about who helped me so much after my surgery — invited me to go with her. I like the church. The pastor has good messages and they have an active singles group. Lately I've started to get more involved with them. I think it's helped some to not feel so alone." She couldn't contain a smile as she added, "One of the guys has started to show an interest in me, but I'm trying to discourage him. There's no way I can get involved again."

She hesitated a moment. "Is Troy seeing anyone?"

Anne flashed a mischievous grin.

"I have noticed the last week or so Mary Ann is starting to

cozy up to him."

"That girl always was jealous of me. I know she had her eye on him even the first day he came to church. I'm not surprised she's trying to sink her claws in him now. Is he...does he return her advances?"

"Kari Lynn, give the man more credit than that. He's polite, but anyone can see he isn't the least interested in her. You know he would get back with you in a second if you gave him half a chance."

"In a way I wish he would find someone. He needs a woman who can give him the family he wants. That someone just can never be me."

Time hung heavy on Troy's hands. More times than he cared to count, he found himself thinking of Kari Lynn. He no longer stopped at The Coffee Hut for a quick cup of coffee. The place held too many memories of time spent there with her. Whenever he saw a woman with long, blond hair walking down the street he had to bite his tongue to keep from calling out. They all reminded him of her.

The first couple of months he avoided the Sunday school class, although he still went to the worship service. It was easier to avoid his friends if he was in the midst of the large congregation. It was hard to try to explain why Kari Lynn wasn't there.

One Sunday he met Amy, one of her friends, in the hallway.

"I haven't seen Kari Lynn in a long time. Is she going somewhere else? She never missed a Sunday before."

He hesitated, not knowing what to say.

"I think she is going someplace else right now."

A look of surprise covered Amy's face.

"Why? I thought she liked it here. Did we insult her or something? It's not like her to stay away."

"No. She...we... we aren't seeing each other anymore, and I think she feels uncomfortable being around her old friends." He frowned. "Especially me."

"I'm sorry to hear that. I expected to hear wedding bells. What happened?"

"We just had some issues come between us."

He turned toward the sanctuary.

"I see the service is about to start. I better go find a seat." He lifted his hand in a brief wave. "See you around, Amy."

He tried to fill his empty hours with activities, but it didn't seem to help him forget. A couple of new clients gave him extra work and the additional hours he needed to put in some days were a welcome diversion.

The gym helped some. He knew the exercise was good for him, and the strenuous workout helped keep his mind away from her. It felt good to take out some of his frustration with the weights. He hadn't gotten enough exercise when he was spending so much time with her, so maybe it was a good thing to devote more effort to getting his body back in shape. His muscles were getting a little flabby.

His friend, Chad, invited him out for coffee several times and they discussed his situation. It was helpful to have someone to talk to he knew would respect his confidence and offer some insight.

Social events were still uncomfortable. Without Kari Lynn at his side it just wasn't the same. And he wasn't sure he wanted to face the questions he knew people were bound to ask. Several inquired where she was and he was always hard pressed to come up with an answer. He had no idea it would be so difficult.

The Sunday school class planned a social get together and he debated if he should attend. He and Kari Lynn never missed one of their events before. So many of the group were paired off, and he knew this would only make him miss her more than ever.

Sunday after church he met Chad in the hallway.

"Going to the social Friday?"

"I haven't decided yet. It's a little uncomfortable without Kari Lynn."

"I understand how you feel. But you do need to be careful. You don't want to isolate yourself from all your friends. It isn't healthy. We need other believers around us. We aren't meant to go this Christian life alone."

"I know. I miss spending time with the others. You would think I would be used to life without her by now and feel like socializing, but it's just not the same. I know it's over six months, but I'm still a little raw around the edges."

He ran his fingers through his hair and looked down at the floor a moment.

"I still haven't gotten used to getting on with life without her. Guess I need to learn how to spend time alone. That's probably part of what got us in trouble. We neglected associating with others and spent too much time just the two of us."

"Could be. Sometimes too much of a good thing isn't good. Remember I'm keeping you in my prayers. I know this isn't easy for you, but God can see you through. And who knows? One of these days she may realize she needs you as much as you want her. Don't give up hope yet. I know God has someone for you. If by some chance it isn't Kari Lynn, then there's no way the two of you would want to get married anyway."

"I know. That thought has crossed my mind more than

once. I'm just not able to see that He has different plans for us. I am praying a lot about our situation and just need to wait to see what He has in mind."

"You and I need to get together more often. I know you're hurting, and sometimes it helps to share what you're going through. How about a round of golf next Saturday and lunch afterward? Anne said she has something planned with Kari Lynn then. Might do you good to get out a little, take your mind off what you can't have."

"Sounds good. I haven't been on the course in quite a while. I'm sure I've gotten a little rusty."

Just then Anne came down the hall toward them.

"Hi Troy. How are you doing? I talked to Kari Lynn the other day and I think she's not so sure this splitting up was the right thing to do. But she's sticking to her guns, convinced it isn't fair to you if she marries you."

"I know. Well, I better let you folks be on your way. See you Saturday, Chad."

It was difficult to see Chad and Anne together. He and Kari Lynn spent so much time with them before. It only served to make him miss her all the more.

More often than he wanted, thoughts of her came to mind. What is she doing? Is she happy? He wondered if she regretted breaking everything off. If only he could talk to her, but he wouldn't force the issue. If and when she changed her mind he was ready to take up where they left off. Until then there was nothing he could do.

chapter 15

Several months later.

The aroma of fresh coffee filled Troy's senses as he fought a cold November wind to pull the door of The Coffee Hut open. He hadn't been here in a long time, but the smell of his favorite brew when he happened to walk past drew him through the door. As he stepped inside the crowded room his mind was filled with visions of the many times spent here with Kari Lynn in the past. Perhaps this wasn't such a good idea after all.

As he settled into a chair at one of the tables, his eye caught sight of a woman in a booth at the back of the room. Her back was toward him, but he would recognize that blond hair anywhere.

It couldn't be her. He shook his head, remembering the last time he mistook someone for Kari Lynn. That helped him turn away. Just because the place reminded him of her didn't mean it was. It was only his imagination playing tricks on him again.

The woman stepped out of the booth and turned so he could see her face.

Kari Lynn!

He smiled and jumped to his feet. "I didn't expect to see you here. It's good to see you."

Her face was an expressionless mask and he was afraid she

was going to walk past without speaking.

"Hello, Troy," she murmured without looking at him. She hesitated a moment as though wanting to stop, yet it was easy to see she wasn't comfortable.

Tension thick enough to cut filled the air between them. He didn't know what to say. They hadn't seen each other since Chad and Anne's wedding nine months ago, but by her actions and the tone of her voice it didn't appear she'd changed her mind about him.

He motioned to the chair across the table.

"If you're not in a hurry why don't you join me?"

She looked down at the floor a moment as though undecided. Then she slowly took a step toward the chair he indicated and lowered herself to the edge.

"How are you? You're looking well."

She just stared at a stain on the table top and an uncomfortable silence fell between them.

Before things got too uncomfortable he spoke. "Are things starting to get better for you?"

Again she made no comment so he went on.

"I've done a lot of soul searching these last months. I didn't know how to get over what happened. I still felt so guilty about what we did."

Her head jerked up then.

"Please don't bring that up again."

A frown marred the beautiful face and a tinge of irritation edged her voice. She rubbed her finger over the spot on the table several times.

"I'm trying to forget what I did and get on with my life." A lopsided grin appeared, although she still didn't look at him. "I'm afraid I'm not doing a very good job of it though."

He leaned across the table and put a tentative hand over hers, surprised when she didn't pull it away.

"Let me tell you what helped me more than anything else I tried to do."

The waitress set a cup of coffee on the table in front of him. "Will there be anything else?"

He motioned for her to wait a moment.

"You want something to drink, Kari Lynn?"

"No thanks. I just had one of their huge cappuccinos. You know, the ones you used to buy me..."

Her gaze dropped to the hands she'd placed in her lap, her fingers nervously rubbing each other. It was obvious she wasn't comfortable talking about their past.

"I guess that will be all," he told the waitress, and then turned his attention once more to the woman across the table.

"I don't know how you drink those things. Give me a plain old cup of java with a dash of sugar and I'm happy."

He shoved the cup aside and looked at Kari Lynn for several moments.

"I'd like to tell you about a place I visited a couple of months ago that was a tremendous help to finally get over what happened. It's in Chattanooga, Tennessee, a place called the National Memorial for the Unborn. I think if you went there it would help you be able to put everything behind you. I know it did for me. I'd be glad to take you sometime if you want."

"What kind of place is it?" she asked, although she didn't sound all that interested.

"It's a place where people can go to remember their children lost to abortion."

"Don't even bother telling me about it."

She pushed her chair back and started to get up. Troy

caught her arm before she could walk away.

"Please don't leave until you have a chance to hear me out. I really want to help you."

She dropped back to the edge of the chair, although her expression told him she wasn't interested in what he had to say.

Troy waited until he had as much of her attention as she seemed willing to give.

"It's a place where you can grieve your loss and leave a tribute if you want to identify the baby as a person. Like the one we never had a chance to know. I know it helped me find some sort of closure to all of this, and I know it could do the same for you."

He looked across the table, willing her to understand.

"I tried to make myself believe it was over, but I knew it wasn't. It was still difficult for me to find the end of that chapter in my life. I just wasn't able to put it away. When I went to the memorial I was able to finally put our baby to rest. Now I can go on. I'm certain this place could do that for you as well."

"I don't want to go. I finally found as much peace in my life as I'll probably ever find and I don't want that all destroyed again. I wish you wouldn't bring it all up. I just want to try to forget it happened."

"I know. I wanted to forget it myself, but I knew it wouldn't just go away by trying to close my mind to it. It was still there in the back of my memory, haunting me whenever I let it."

He paused and took a deep breath.

"By recognizing our baby as a living human being it did help me heal. I am now at peace."

He thought for a minute before continuing.

"It's like when anyone dies. We put up a marker so we can visit it and remember that person. It's the same for our baby. I put a plaque on the wall at the memorial to identify our little one as a real person. Before that there was nothing, nothing to remind me of our child except my unpleasant memories."

Kari Lynn pushed her chair back again, but remained seated. She fidgeted with the crease in her slacks.

"I don't want to go. I don't want to be reminded again of what I did."

"I know it won't be easy. It was difficult for me. But I think it would help you get over everything. It did me."

He pulled a napkin from the holder on the table.

"Let me give you the website of the memorial. That way you can check it out for yourself and see what others say about it."

He jotted down the website and handed it to her.

"You remember Bill and Karen Dodds from church, don't you?"

She nodded.

"Bill's the one who told me about it. He said Karen had an abortion several years ago and she still had problems dealing with it. It was their visit to the memorial that showed her God loved her no matter what she did. They said it was a great help for what they were going through. They encouraged me to go, saying it would help me deal with everything."

Kari Lynn took the napkin and stuffed it in her jacket pocket.

"I'll think about it. But I'm not promising anything."

He stood when she got to her feet.

"It was good to see you again." He hesitated a moment, then added, "I've missed you."

She didn't reply.

He watched as she turned and walked toward the entrance. The door closed behind her and he returned to his seat. His mind was still on the brief encounter when he picked up the coffee cup. After one sip of the now cold beverage he shoved it aside.

As soon as she returned home, Kari Lynn went to her computer. If only she could be as comfortable with everything as Troy seemed to be.

When the website came up she wasn't sure she wanted to look at it. She was trying her best to get over what happened and didn't want to bring it all up again.

Drawing in a deep breath, she let herself scan the information on the website. It did sound interesting. As difficult as she knew it would be, maybe it would be good for her to go. Although she still had doubts, if it helped Troy get over the pain perhaps it would help her as well.

Her phone rang a few days and she was taken by surprise when she heard Troy. She hadn't talked to him on the phone in such a long time she hardly recognized his voice.

"Did you check out that website I gave you?"

"Yes, I did. It does look good, but I still don't know if I want to go. I don't think I can I face it all again."

"Why don't I meet you at The Coffee Hut a little later and we can talk about it some more? I want to help you get over this."

She chewed on her thumbnail and gave it some thought. Did she want to see him again? It was kind of nice to see him the other day, even though it was a shock. But she was afraid if she saw any more of him she might forget her resolve that their life together was over.

"I'm waiting for an answer." Troy chuckled. "I'm assuming since you didn't say otherwise, it means you're agreeable."

Kari Lynn pulled in a deep breath. It was against her better judgment, but finally she answered. "I suppose it would be all right."

"Good. I'll pick you up in, say, thirty minutes."

"No, I'll walk. It's only a block from here."

"Okay. I'll see you there in a half hour."

Troy was waiting just inside the door when she walked into the coffee shop. He smiled and led her to the booth at the back of the room. They visited over coffee and her favorite cappuccino for nearly two hours before she told him she needed to get home. He had steered the conversation as much as possible away from their problems in the past, for which she was grateful. But he did bring up the possibility of a trip to the memorial. She surprised herself by agreeing to go with him the following weekend.

Kari Lynn stared out the window of their rental car as Troy drove the short distance from the airport to the memorial. She wished she could just fade into oblivion and not have to go to this place he was taking her.

They pulled up in front of an unfamiliar building and she squirmed in her seat. Knowing what it represented, she couldn't keep a shudder from going through her at the sight of the place. Although it looked harmless enough, there was no way she could go inside. It would bring all the grief and pain flooding back again.

Troy helped her from the car, took her hand, and led her toward the memorial. She took a few steps, then stopped.

"I can't go in," she whispered. "I just can't. I don't want to have everything brought back when I have finally attained a measure of peace."

Concern for her was written all over his face and it made

her uncomfortable.

"I know it will be difficult at first, but you do need some kind of closure. It was hard for me when I first came. But it isn't what you think. Once you step inside the door you'll feel the comfort the place has to offer."

Turning away, she started back toward the car.

"I'm sorry. I just can't face it right now."

He followed her.

"Did you look at the website some more?" he asked as he opened her door.

"Yes, I read everything they had. It sounds good, but I just don't think I'm able to go inside." She looked up at him. "Too many bad memories I don't want to be reminded of again. Let's just go to the motel."

"If you're sure."

She nodded.

He closed her door and got in the driver's seat.

"Maybe it would be better if we came later. I don't want to force you if you're not ready. The motel is just a few blocks from here. We can get settled in our rooms and get something to eat. We'll see how you feel by then."

While they were eating their lunch he mentioned a park he noticed across the street. When he suggested they check it out, she agreed. Anything to avoid going to that awful place.

The sun warmed them as they walked along the paths. Colorful autumn flowers bloomed in profusion in beds throughout the park.

Thoughts ran wild as they walked hand in hand. Feelings of guilt and pain were still buried not far below the surface of her mind. If only this memorial could take away some of the grief she carried. She had hoped over time it wouldn't be quite such a burden, but it hadn't seemed to lessen much. At least she was able to forgive herself for what she did, as well as Troy. And she was assured God forgave her, although it still bothered her that she grieved Him so.

She couldn't help smiling when she remembered how excited she was when she found out she was pregnant. Although, she wished she and Troy were married before it happened. Her arms ached from wanting to hold her child, to hold it for even one second. But she was never given that opportunity. There wasn't a day went by she didn't remember she chose to end the life of the innocent little one. Maybe this place would be good for her. She hoped so.

They walked all the paths in the park, but she hadn't enjoyed many of the beautiful flowers. Her mind was too occupied with other things.

Finally she turned to Troy.

"I think I'm ready to see what we came for. If you think it will be good for me to go, then I'm sure it is. I know you wouldn't bring me all this way if you didn't think it was the right thing."

Her knees felt weak when she saw Troy's familiar smile and felt him squeeze her hand.

"If you're certain. I don't want to force you to do something you're not ready for. We can walk a while longer if you want. The memorial is open twenty-four hours, so it's no hurry."

"I think I'm as ready as I ever will be. I just want to put everything behind me so I can go on. If you think this place can do that for me, then I suppose I should go."

Even though she couldn't look at him, she was aware of his concern as he helped her into the car. In a few minutes he parked in the lot of the memorial.

"Are you okay?" he asked as he opened the door for her.

She pulled in a deep breath and nodded, unable to find her voice to reply. Forcing her eyes toward the place they had come, she looked around, taking in her surroundings.

Black, wrought iron fence between brick pillars surrounded a courtyard in front of the building. Brick columns stood on either side of the entrance. Wrought iron gates were swung wide, encouraging visitors to come inside. Maybe this wouldn't be so bad after all. It looked harmless enough.

When they reached the gate she stopped. A plaque on one of the pillars caught her attention and she paused to read it.

"The glory of this latter
house shall be greater
than that of the former, saith
the Lord of hosts; and in
this place will I give peace."
Haggai 2:9

Welcome...the gates and doors
of the National Memorial for
the Unborn are always open...
please enter in peace.

She pulled in a deep breath and took a hesitant step through the gate that brought them into the courtyard. Several large trees dotted the landscape.

"You all right?"

"Yes, I...I think so," she whispered as she took a couple more steps.

Beyond the rock covered courtyard stood a building with

floor to ceiling windows all across the front. To the left of the entrance gate was a large boulder. A plaque leaning against the base told the history of the memorial. She glanced at it, but what it said looked much the same as what she read on the website, so she didn't stop. A white marble sculpture of a baby cradled in the arms of an angel sat atop a pedestal in the center of the courtyard. It reminded her of her own baby, and she had to look away.

Steps to the right led to a garden filled with trees and flowering plants and she considered going to see what was there. At least it was outside. It might not be as bad as going inside the building. But Troy tugged at her hand and guided her toward the glass doors of the building.

They stepped inside a long narrow room. As she looked around, her taut muscles began to relax. This wasn't so bad. At least not yet.

A wall of dark gray granite at the front of the building drew her attention. Attached to it were a multitude of small brass plaques. A family speaking in hushed voices stood looking at one of the plates. Another young couple stood nearby crying.

Troy guided her across the room. An array of toys — dolls, baseballs and gloves, and other mementos — crowded a ledge part way up the granite wall. Her heart clenched when she saw a young woman weep as she placed a teddy bear among the other toys.

As she came closer she was able to read some of the words written on the small plaques. She couldn't stop tears from running down her face as she read the inscriptions, tributes to babies who, like her own, never had a chance to experience life. She was grateful for the arm Troy kept around her waist.

He paused as they moved along the wall. Tears flowed down

his face as he pointed to a small brass plaque in front of him. Kari Lynn moved her lips as she read the words on the metal plate.

KARI LYNN & TROY'S ANGEL
One day we will hold you.
Forgive us.

She looked at him, her mind racing with questions.

"It's for our baby," he whispered.

He brushed at the tears still running down his face.

"I had it made when I came here before. I hope you like what it says. We can have them make another one if you want to say something different."

His arms went around her and he pulled her close. She buried her face in his shoulder.

"It's perfect," she whispered. "I couldn't say it any better."

She turned back and traced her finger across the words.

"Our little angel. She's with Jesus now, isn't she?"

He nodded.

She never knew if the baby she carried for such a brief time was a boy or a girl. Since she always hoped to have a baby girl someday, it seemed natural for her to refer to the child they conceived as she.

"I'll be able to hold her in my arms when I get to heaven, won't I?" she asked as she read the words inscribed on the plaque again.

Her arms ached to hold her child now.

"I just wish I didn't have to wait that long."

"Yes, Kari Lynn, she's waiting for us," Troy whispered in her ear. "One day we will see her and be able to tell her ourselves how sorry we are for what we did."

Unbelief flooded her mind and she turned to look up at him, suddenly horrified.

"Troy, I can't believe we did such an awful thing to our baby. Will she even be able to forgive us? I'm not sure I want to face her when I get to heaven. I don't know what I'll tell her. I can never begin to tell her how sorry I am for what I did to her."

He didn't reply. Apparently he had no answers, but she knew he would have to agree, it wouldn't be easy.

She gazed at the brass plate for several minutes, sometimes tears blurring her vision so she couldn't make out the words. Troy's presence next to her gave her the strength to remain.

After several minutes she bowed her head and poured out her heart to God in little more than a whisper.

"Oh, God, forgive me for the things I did to grieve You. Please give me freedom from the guilt and pain I still feel over what I did. Hold my baby close, Jesus. Make sure she knows I love her and will see her one day. Then I'll be able to hold her for the rest of eternity. Tell her to try to find it in her little heart to forgive me for what I did and for never getting to know her. Tell her that her mommy loves her very much."

"Let her know her daddy loves her too," Troy whispered. "And I'm sorry, so very sorry."

She turned toward Troy in the arms he still had wrapped around her. His hand stroked her hair as she sobbed into his shoulder.

Finally she raised her face toward him.

"I believe God is beginning to remove the guilt and pain I carried for so long. I know I will never stop being sorry for what I did, but at least I won't have to carry the load any longer. Thanks for bringing me, Troy. Thank you for caring enough to invite me to come here."

"I think it was good for both of us. Although I knew God forgave me, I still struggled with what I did. When I came here I was able to identify her as a living being, and that allowed me to begin to be at peace with it."

"I believe I'm ready to go. I think I have finally put my baby to rest. Now I'll be able to go on."

Before turning to leave she took one last look at the small plaque, their memorial to the baby she never knew. She traced her finger across the letters and whispered, "Goodbye, little angel. Sleep in peace in the arms of Jesus."

Taking Troy's hand in hers she let him lead her across the room. "I know our little angel is at peace. And at long last so am I."

He squeezed her hand.

"Are you glad you came?"

"Yes, I am glad you brought me. It was difficult to be reminded of it all again, but I'm glad you were thoughtful enough to bring me."

She grinned at him through her tears.

"You know, I still didn't want to come. When it came time to get on the plane I was ready to turn around and run home. Even when we first got here I didn't think I could go in and let myself be reminded of everything again. But if I hadn't come I would have missed the chance to put our little angel to rest."

❀❀❀

Sleep refused to come for Kari Lynn as she lay in bed in her motel room staring at the ceiling. She was glad Troy brought her to the memorial. At last she could now identify the baby she carried for such a short time as a living person. Although she still wished it never happened, at least now she felt at peace.

She remembered seeing several letters at the memorial people had written to babies they had aborted. A thought came to her. Slipping from bed she made her way to the desk where she found paper and a pen and began writing.

Dear little angel,

Forgive me for what I did to you. I think about you every day and wish I could hold you in my arms. I don't know why I listened to your daddy. I could have brought you into the world and raised you by myself if he didn't want anything to do with us. But don't blame him. He was only doing what he thought was right at the time.

I love you, little angel. I'm so sorry. I can't wait to see you someday in Heaven. Then I'll be able to hold you for all of eternity.

Please forgive me. Rest peacefully in the arms of Jesus until I can hold you myself.

Love,
Mommy

She laid the letter beside her purse. They could stop at the memorial on their way to the airport the next morning and leave it with the others. Maybe they might even have time to buy a little doll to leave with the letter.

This decided, she slipped back into bed, swiping at the tears that insisted on coming. She wished she and Troy could return to the relationship they had before, but she knew she could never marry him. She wondered if he still loved her as much as he had. But even if he did, she knew he would never be satisfied in a marriage with no children.

"Oh God, why did this have to happen? We should have been satisfied to wait until marriage. But instead of waiting for Your leading we took things in our own hands. We could have had such a wonderful life together, but that's all destroyed now."

She made no attempt to stop the flow of tears dampening her pillow.

"I wish You would have taken my life right along with my baby, God. Then I wouldn't have to face a future without Troy. At least then I could be with my little angel."

chapter 16

During the weeks following their trip to The National Memorial for the Unborn, Troy and Kari Lynn met several times at The Coffee Hut. She enjoyed spending time with him again. He seemed to try to make their time together casual, and she appreciated that. It was as though they were nothing more than friends meeting over a cup of coffee, not someone with whom she once shared an intimate relationship. She looked forward to these times with him again.

One unseasonably warm day the end of April she was surprised to receive a phone call from him while she was at work.

"Hey, Kari Lynn, how about dinner at my place tonight? I stopped at the store on the way home from work yesterday and picked up two of the biggest, juiciest steaks they had. You know no one can grill a steak better than me."

"I wouldn't brag if I were you. You never tasted the ones Dad used to cook over the campfire up at the cabin. Now those were good."

He chuckled. "I'll put mine up against his any day."

"We'll see. Maybe we can have a contest some time and see who does cook the best one."

"We might just do that. Well, I'll pick you up at your apartment on my way home from work. See you later."

A multitude of emotions skittered through Kari Lynn when she heard Troy's familiar knock — anticipation, excitement, some apprehension, and even a nagging doubt if it was in her best interest to get involved with him again.

"You're early," she said when she opened the door. "I didn't expect you this soon."

"Things were slow today so I left a little early." She didn't miss the twinkle in his eye when he added, "I couldn't wait for you to sink your teeth into that steak. Ready?"

"Yes, let's go. But remember, I'll be comparing yours with the ones my dad used to cook. Unless yours are something extra spectacular they won't even come close to his."

"I'm not worried," he countered with a grin.

When they walked into his apartment she tossed her jacket over a chair and started to follow him toward the kitchen.

"Oops, can't have anyone out here with me."

He turned her around and shooed her back into the living room.

Shrugging her shoulders, she made her way to the couch. As she pulled her long legs under her she reached for the TV remote. Might as well watch the evening news as long as she was banished from the kitchen.

Fifteen minutes later Troy came into the room. He pushed the door to the balcony open while balancing a plate of meat, tools for the grill, and seasoning containers in his hands.

"Not that I don't enjoy your company," he tossed over his shoulder before sliding the door closed with his foot. "I just don't want to give away any of my secrets. I'll be in to join you shortly."

A few minutes later he settled on the couch next to her.

"Shouldn't you be out there keeping an eye on your steaks to make sure they don't burn? Dad always left the rest of the meal up to Mom so he could devote his entire attention to the meat."

"Guess that's the difference between his and mine."

A commercial came on and he looked at his watch.

"Be right back. Time to check on progress."

Just as the news broadcast ended he walked into the living room. He bowed before her and held out his hand.

"Dinner is served, milady. May I escort you to the table?"

She attempted to stifle a giggle, but it managed to sneak past the hand she put to her mouth.

"What is this, some kind of fancy restaurant?"

The solemn expression on his face brought another chuckle.

However, she wasn't prepared for the sight that greeted her when he led her into the kitchen. As the swinging doors closed behind her, her breath caught.

A light blue table cloth covered the small, round table. The flicker of candles in the center created a romantic ambiance. Several red roses floating in a bowl of water emanated a soft fragrance, and she was unable to resist the temptation to lower her nose and inhale the delicate scent.

Troy pulled out her chair and helped her be seated.

Seconds later he set a warmed plate before her. Her eyes flew open. The biggest steak she ever saw, done to perfection, emitted an aroma she could hardly resist. A baked potato wrapped in foil nestled beside the meat. Next a tossed salad appeared beside her plate.

"I'm impressed," she said in an awed whisper.

After asking the blessing, he turned his attention to her.

"Well," he asked, "what do you think?"

"I'm spellbound!" She looked up at him and smiled. "I didn't know you had it in you." She motioned toward the table. "Everything is beautiful. This is just like eating at an expensive restaurant. And the food smells heavenly. You thought of everything."

He accepted her compliments with a smile, his face coloring slightly. Then he nodded toward her plate.

"I wasn't talking about the table. I mean what do you think of my steak?"

She picked up her knife and fork and cut a small bite of the meat. After putting it in her mouth she closed her eyes and let it roll around on her tongue.

"It's good."

"Is that all you can say, 'it's good'?"

"It's delicious." She took another bite. "It is good, real good. I would say you could give Dad some stiff competition."

"Do your folks still come up to the cabin for the summer? We need to have a contest someday."

"They don't come for all summer anymore, but they do come for a few weeks most years."

"Next time they come we need to have a cook off. You will be the judge." He grinned. "You'll get to marry whichever one of us wins."

His mention of marriage took her by surprise, but she was certain he was only joking so she decided to play along.

"You're pretty confident, aren't you?" she asked as she cut another bite of meat. "Besides, it isn't fair. Dad's already married, so I would have to choose yours even if it isn't the best."

"That's the idea." Troy smiled and cut into his own steak.

She removed the foil from around the potato and applied

butter and sour cream. There was no way she was going to go any further in that direction.

They ate for a couple minutes in silence.

"I didn't realize you were such a good cook," she said as she picked up a forkful of her salad. "Oh, the meals up at the cabin when you came up there were good, but they were nothing compared to this feast. Everything is delicious." She waved her hand over the food in front of her. "But how you expect me to ever be able to eat all of this is beyond me. This steak is HUGE!"

Troy refused her offer to help clean up the kitchen when they finished eating.

"I can do that later," he told her as he led her toward the living room. "Tonight was kind of a celebration dinner. I wanted to let you know I would like to continue our relationship. That is if it's alright with you. I have missed you and would like to start over again, only this time in a way pleasing to God."

She nibbled on her thumb nail a minute. How should she answer? Yes, she missed him, too. And she knew she still loved him, had never stopped.

"I won't rush you," he said quietly. "We'll just get to know each other again and see where it goes from there."

Thoughts chased each other through her mind. She wasn't sure if it would be right, all things considered. Confusion clouded her mind for several minutes and she felt Troy's gaze on her.

"I think I might like that," she murmured. "I have enjoyed our time together at The Coffee Hut the last few weeks. And this evening."

A few hours later Troy drove her back to her apartment and accompanied her to her door.

"Thank you for tonight," he said as she put her key in the lock. "It was like old times again."

His eyes closed a moment before he looked at her again. "Like those days before…"

Although he didn't finish his sentence, she knew what he was thinking. It was still difficult to forget those days, much less talk about them. She wanted to put it all out of her mind.

She closed the door behind him, then leaned against it until she heard the last of his soft footsteps down the carpeted hallway.

Yes, tonight did seem like old times. The good times. She had to admit she did miss him after she told him they couldn't see each other anymore. That was over a year ago. Now she was beginning to regret her choice to break up with him, although she still knew it was the best thing to do at the time. For both of them. Maybe it was time for them to get back together again.

Making her way toward the bedroom, she sat on the edge of the bed. She dropped her head in her hands and turned her heart toward God.

"Show us Your plan for the future, Lord. Troy and I enjoyed such good times together. I know I could never love anyone the way I love him. Tonight felt so right. But I never want to step ahead of Your plans again."

chapter 17

One warm, June Saturday Troy called and asked if she would like to go to Como Park. She always enjoyed it there; there was so much to see and do. She agreed the day outdoors would be good for her and promised a picnic lunch so they could spend the entire day.

The sun was warm as they visited the various things of interest the park offered. She reveled in the feel of him beside her as they meandered along. How she loved being with him.

Her hand found his and her fingers seemed to have a mind of their own as they laced themselves between his. His hand squeezed hers in response. This is where she wanted to be. Right here beside him for the rest of her life.

Later, as she was cleaning up the remains of their lunch, she glanced in his direction. She couldn't miss the thoughtful expression on his face and wondered what he was thinking, but didn't have long to wait.

After putting the picnic things in the car, he led her to a secluded bench. When they were settled, he turned toward her.

"Kari Lynn, it's so good to spend time with you like this again. I really missed you those months we were apart."

She turned to look at him, wondering where this was going.

Yes, she had to agree she did enjoy being with him too. The last weeks were almost like old times.

Tingles of electricity shot up her spine when his hand found hers. His fingers caressed hers for a moment.

"You know I love you, have loved you for a long time. I'm also certain you love me."

Her breath caught in her throat. She was afraid she knew what was coming next and she wasn't sure she wanted to go there.

"I realize we had some rough spots in our relationship earlier. And we haven't seen much of each other until the last few months. However nothing that happened in the past has dimmed my love for you. If anything, it has only grown stronger because of what we went through. I believe even our separation was good for us. It gave us time to think and pray about what lies ahead in our future. I know I spent a lot of time in prayer, something I missed there for a few months."

He smiled at her, and she was certain now she knew what he was going to say.

"We talked about marriage in the past. I think it was something we both wanted, but I never actually asked you to marry me."

Holding her breath, she waited for him to go on. She had no idea how she was going to answer the question she knew he was about to ask.

"Kari Lynn, will you marry me? Will you be my wife?"

Her voice seemed to have escaped for several minutes and she pulled her hand away, not able to even look at him.

"I…I'm sorry. I…I'm afraid I can't," she whispered at last.

His body tensed beside her and she didn't dare look at him. It was obvious he was shocked by her answer. And hurt.

Several seconds went past and she felt him staring at her. She let her gaze flit around the park. Anything to avoid looking at him.

"You…you can't?" he finally managed to ask in a strangled whisper. "Why not? Did I do something? Is there someone else?"

"No, it's not you. And there is no one else. There never will be. It's me. It wouldn't be fair to you if I married you."

When he turned her face toward his she couldn't miss the confused — and hurt — expression covering his face.

"What do you mean, it wouldn't be fair?"

His brow drew in a knot as he searched her face.

"Are you saying you don't love me?"

There was no way she could look into that face she loved any longer. Pain etched every inch of his handsome features. Rubbing her palms up and down her jean clad thighs she tried to think of something to say. Anything to relieve his pain. And her own.

She stared across the park, afraid to look at him.

"No, I'm not saying I don't love you because I do." She ignored the trail of tears she knew were making their way down her face. "That's what makes this so difficult."

"I don't understand. If you love me, then why you can't marry me? There has to be a reason."

He reached for her hand but she pulled it away.

"I have prayed and prayed about this, and feel at peace this is what God wants, for us to be together."

He slid to the edge of the bench and turned toward her. She knew he was looking at her, but she couldn't look at him.

"What is it? I don't understand."

After looking down at his lap for a moment he lifted his head. With a gentle hand he turned her face so she had to look at him. He looked directly into her eyes. She dropped her gaze to the top button of his shirt, not able to look into those troubled, confused green eyes. It hurt too much.

"I thought you forgave me."

A tear slipped from his eye and he wiped it away before gathering her into his arms.

"Don't let our past continue to come between us. I still wish it never happened, but it's over. We can't carry our mistakes with us forever. I love you, Kari Lynn. I love you even more now than I did before."

He held her for several minutes.

"Please tell me what's wrong," he whispered. "I want to know."

It tore at her heart to see the tears that streamed down his face.

"It's nothing you did. It's me. I just can't marry you, as much as I want to."

She watched people stroll along the paths for several minutes. Thoughts she couldn't stop whirled through her mind.

"I suppose it was wrong for me not to say something to you before, but I love you so much I wanted to be with you all the time. I guess I never stopped to think it would one day come to this. Perhaps I let myself believe we could go on the way we were, that we would just be friends. I know that wasn't fair to you, but I didn't want to give you up. I'm sorry. I know I was being selfish. I didn't stop to take your feelings into consideration."

She stared at the hands she had clasped together in her lap. Some kind of explanation needed to be given, but she didn't know what to say.

"I never wanted it to come to this. Can you ever forgive me?"

She was aware of Troy looking at her for several seconds. When she did look up at him, incomprehension was written all over his face.

"You say you love me and wish you could marry me. So why can't you? There has to be some reason."

He continued to look into her eyes until she had to turn

away. She couldn't bear the pain she saw on his face. She clasped her hands tighter in her lap and fastened her gaze on them.

"I suppose I do owe you an explanation, but it's difficult."

Tears she wasn't able to stop ran down her face.

"I know how much it means to you to have a family, how much you love children. You used to talk about it so often."

A weak smile managed to break through the tears.

"Remember all those times you told me you wanted a dozen kids? Oh, I know you were just joking about having exactly twelve, but I know you want more than one."

She pulled in a deep breath, still unable to look at him.

"You know I can never have children. I can never give you the family you want. Not even one little one. It wouldn't be fair for me to marry you when I know I can never bless your home with the babies you want. I'm sorry. I really am. I wish things could be different, but I don't see how they can."

His hand touched her chin and he tilted her face again and looked into her eyes.

"Is that all that's keeping you from marrying me, the fact that you can never give me children?"

Unbelief covered his face. He shook his head as though he couldn't believe what she just told him.

"Yes. It's the only thing."

"Don't let that stand in the way of our getting married. I love you. There's nothing I want more than to have you beside me for the rest of my life. It's you I want, you I love, you I want to share my life with. If we never have a family it doesn't make any difference. After all, I'm the one to blame for your inability to have children. I could never hold that against you."

"Oh, you say that now, but someday I know you will be disappointed when there are no little ones running around our house. I know how much you love them. You would never be satisfied with a childless home."

"Don't try to second guess me, Kari Lynn. It's you who would make me happy, you alone."

Tears continued to stream down her face, but she made no attempt to stop them.

"As much as I hate the thought of losing you, I think it would be best if you found someone who can give you a family, the family you want and deserve."

His jaw dropped as he sat back, a look of utter surprise and disbelief written clearly on his face.

"Kari Lynn, what are you saying? I don't want anyone else. It's you I want to spend the rest of my life with."

He hesitated a moment.

"You say that's the only thing that stands in the way of our getting married. You're sure it's not what happened in the past still coming between us."

She shook her head. "No. That's the only reason. I have dealt with my past, as much as I despise what I did. But I can't marry you when I know I can never give you the family I know you want so much."

He stared off into the distance for several minutes. Finally he turned to her.

"There's always adoption. If some day we decide we want a family we can always —"

"No!" She leaped to her feet, shaking her head forcefully. "I could never adopt. It's out of the question."

Troy's eyes blinked as he looked at her. His surprise at her vehement reaction was all over his face.

"What's wrong with adoption? Families do it all the time."

"I know other people do. But I could never adopt someone

else's child." She stamped her foot for emphasis. "Don't even think about it."

His brow wrinkled in obvious confusion.

"Why not? There are lots of children who need a good home. If it weren't for people like us who want to be loving parents, what would happen to them?"

Shaking her head again, she dropped wearily back on the bench. "There may be nothing wrong with it for someone else, but I can never do it."

He placed one hand on hers, and with the other lifted her chin. "Kari Lynn, please look at me. Tell me why you are so against adoption."

"I could never love another woman's child," she whispered as she stared across his shoulder. "I can't take another person's castaway and pretend it's mine, that's all."

Tears came again and she swiped at her eyes.

"I want my own children. I want to feel a baby grow inside of me, to experience the first kick. I want the privilege of going through the pains of child birth, to hear its first cry, to hold the new born child in my arms."

Her head dropped to his shoulder as her tears continued to flow. "I can never experience any of that now. If I can't have my own, then I don't want another woman's castoff."

Troy was silent for a few minutes before he spoke again.

"I'm sorry. I know that's what every woman wants, to have her own baby. But please don't think of adopted children as castoffs. They're lovable children the same as any other. I'm sure once you held an adopted child in your arms you would love it just as much as if you gave birth to it."

"Never!" Her forehead rubbed across his shirt as she shook her head back and forth. "I could never love some other woman's baby. I'm sorry, but it's the way I am. There's no use to even discuss it anymore."

Troy stared across the park for a minute, then turned to Kari Lynn. "I guess I never told you this before. Not that I tried to hide anything from you," he was quick to add, "but I just never thought about it. The subject never came up before."

His eyes bored deep into hers.

"I'm adopted."

Her breath caught and she felt her mouth drop open.

"It's not something I think about. I don't feel any different than I would if Mom and Dad were my actual birth parents. To me they are my parents. The only ones I have. I couldn't love them more if they conceived me and brought me into the world. And I know they couldn't love me anymore if they had. I never felt like a castaway, and I know my parents never thought of me as such. To them I was their very special child. Both my sister and I were. They never put it into those words, but they made us believe we were special. Perhaps even more so than if they gave us birth."

She pushed herself a few inches away from him.

"That may be the way they felt, but I could never love another woman's baby as my own. I know I couldn't. So don't even talk about it as an option. I'm sorry. I understand you're disappointed, but I don't see how we could possibly get married when we know the way things are."

Troy looked across the park for several minutes before turning to face her again. His gaze searched hers.

"We won't worry now about whether or not we will adopt a family. I just want to be sure the only reason you say you can't marry me is because you feel I will be disappointed when you don't give me children."

"That's the only reason. Our past is over. Although I'm still disappointed it happened, it doesn't stand in the way of our happiness. I wish things could be different, but I know they never can. I would love to give you the dozen babies you want, but I can't give you even one. I know I would never make you happy."

"Let me be the judge of that, Kari Lynn. It's you who will make me happy." He grasped her hands, shaking them as though to emphasize what he was saying. "You and you alone. Yes, I do like children, but they're not what is important to me. Even if none of the things in the past happened, we would never be guaranteed we would have children anyway. No one knows that for certain."

"I know that. But we do know for sure we can never have any. Even though you never told me, I know you would always be disappointed. I would feel guilty when I knew you weren't truly happy." She held his face in her hands, unable to stop the tears streaming down her cheeks.

"I'm sorry, but I think it's better this way. As much as it hurts to see you go, I know this is best for both of us."

Troy drew in a deep breath and let it out again.

"I'm not giving up. Don't give me your final answer now. Pray about it. I will too. Let God show us what He wants for us."

She nodded.

When he got to his feet he helped her from the bench. Together, hand in hand, they strolled along the paths. Neither spoke, and a strained silence fell between them.

Kari Lynn sobbed in the darkness of her room as she clung to her pillow. Her conversation with Troy hung heavy on her mind. Although she wanted to blame God for everything, for shattering her once perfect world, she knew He wasn't to blame.

Sleep evaded her as thoughts continued to soar through her mind. She couldn't help wonder if Troy would really be that disappointed if they never had children. But as much as she tried to convince herself it might work, she knew it never would.

Then her mind drifted to what he said about adoption.

Yes, she knew there was nothing wrong with it. For other people. But she knew she could never hold another woman's child in her arms and pretend it was her own. The very thought repulsed her. Even though her arms ached to hold a baby, they weren't made to accept another woman's castaway. Her heart wasn't large enough to love that sort of child. There was no way she could ever consider adoption, even if it meant she had to give up Troy, the one person in the world who meant more to her than anything.

chapter 18

Kari Lynn and Troy were spending the Fourth of July weekend with her parents at their lake cabin. Memories of her childhood filled her mind.

Saturday evening Troy and Mr. Moore shooed the women out of the cabin. Mischievous grins covered their faces as they gave each other knowing glances. When she demanded an explanation she was told to mind her own business.

Shrugging her shoulders, she picked up the book she'd been reading and started toward the dock.

"Come on, Mom. We don't seem to be wanted here. Why don't we go and enjoy the breeze off the lake?"

Engrossed in the story, she was suddenly brought back to the present by the whiff of an enticing aroma wafting through the air. When she raised her head from her book to see what was causing it, she couldn't believe her eyes.

There stood Troy, bent intently over his charcoal grill. She wasn't aware he even brought it with him. Her dad was nearby, hovering over a fire in the fire pit. She smiled to herself, recalling the day she defended his cooking when Troy surprised her with his great steak dinner. So, the two men were competing to see who did cook the best meat.

She chuckled and turned back to her book. If she let her mind wander she could still taste the steaks her dad used to cook over the open wood fire. They were so good, the slightly smoky flavor accented by the subtle seasoning he seemed to know when and how to apply. Then she remembered the ones Troy grilled that day at his apartment. Although quite different in flavor, his tasted every bit as good as her dad's. She couldn't keep from smiling. It would be a tough competition.

Her stomach was rumbling from the delicious smells by the time she and her mother were summoned to the table. The sight of the food before her made her mouth water.

A large platter held four tantalizing, juicy steaks, all done to perfection. Freshly tossed salads, steaming baked potatoes, and a green bean casserole completed the meal.

The men escorted the women to the table. Kari Lynn smiled up at Troy when he gave her shoulders a squeeze as he helped her with her chair.

Mr. Moore offered a short prayer for the food and then turned to Troy. Both men grinned from ear to ear.

"The time has come, my dear," Troy announced, "for you to decide which of us can cook the best steak. Your father or me?"

He placed a large piece from two of the steaks on her plate.

She glanced at him and then her dad.

"I'm the only judge?" She asked, noticing her mother's empty plate.

"You're the judge." Troy stepped back, a look of triumph on his face. "No one knows whose steak is which except your dad and me."

She couldn't stop the heat of a blush that rose up her face when he grinned at her.

"You do remember the prize for choosing the best steak, don't you?"

Mr. Moore chuckled, and her cheeks grew even warmer. Troy must have told him about the day she defended her dad's cooking.

She looked at the perfectly grilled beef on the plate in front of her. This was going to be a difficult decision. There was no way she would hurt either man's feelings by saying their cooking wasn't as good as the other's. When she looked from one to the other, she couldn't miss the satisfied, confidant smiles on both men's faces. What a difficult position to be in.

Picking up her knife and fork, she cut a small bite from one of the pieces of meat. She closed her eyes, letting it roll over her tongue as the flavor tickled her taste buds. The subtle, smoky flavor transported her back to a day almost twenty-five years ago.

Little Kari Lynn, blond pigtails blowing in the breeze, stood beside her daddy watching his every move. Occasional gusts of wind blew wisps of smoke in her face, causing her eyes to water.

"What's the matter, Kitten? Smoke getting in your eyes?" Daddy asked as she rubbed her eyes with the back of her fists.

She just smiled and moved closer to him.

"Why don't you run up to the cabin and tell Mommy and your brother the steak is almost ready?"

Although reluctant to leave her daddy's side, Kari Lynn ran toward the building as fast as her little legs would carry her.

Troy's voice broke into her daydream. "Ready to compare?"

She knew this had to come from her dad's fire. No other flavor could conjure up such a wonderful memory of her childhood.

Next she cut a bite from the other piece of meat and let this one roll over her taste buds. It was familiar as well. It reminded her of the day Troy surprised her with his wonderful meal. Tears came to her eyes when she remembered how she treated him after the abortion and subsequent surgery.

Why was I so cruel to him? He was hurting too. He needed my support as much as I needed his. I hate the way I treated him, yet he was nothing but kind and loving toward me. I could never find a man better than Troy. I don't deserve his love. I want more than anything to marry him, but if I do, I know I will disappoint him when we never have children. Yet if I don't, he will be just as disappointed.

Her dad's voice broke into her thoughts.

"Well? We're waiting for your decision. The rest of us want to eat too before it gets cold."

She looked from one of the men in her life to the other. Never in a million years would she purposely hurt either one of them. She didn't know how she ever let herself get in this position.

After placing her fork on her plate she looked up, her gaze going from one of the men to the other.

"I'm afraid I have to call it a tie. They're both excellent in my opinion." She motioned to the meat still on the platter in the center of the table. "Taste it for yourself and see if you don't agree."

The rest of them delved into their food. Troy motioned toward the steak she recognized as her dad's cooking.

"Say, this is good. I guess I finally met my match."

"So is yours," Mr. Moore said as he savored a bite from one of the pieces of meat. He smiled across the table at his wife. "Guess it's time for me to retire and let the younger generation take over."

"Let's just say we have more than one cook in the family. I

think there's room for both of you."

Kari Lynn felt the gaze of each of those she loved settle on her. She knew her parents expected she and Troy would soon be man and wife. Conversation flowed around her as she pondered her dilemma.

She wouldn't hurt Troy for the world, yet whatever direction she chose she knew she would be a disappointment to him. If only she could go back to those simpler days when her family spent the summers here at this quiet and peaceful place. If she could only be given a second chance. But life didn't work that way. You only got one chance and prayed you did things right.

Later that evening Troy and Kari Lynn went for a stroll in the moonlight along the lakeshore. She felt him looking at her.

"I was positive you would give my steak first place this afternoon. You did know which was mine, didn't you?"

She glanced up at him. He had such a serious expression on his face, she knew she had done it again. No matter what she did, she couldn't seem to keep from disappointing him.

Troy turned her to face him, then took both her hands in his and flashed a mischievous grin.

"You did remember the reward, didn't you? You would get to marry the winner."

Her shoulders sagged in relief when she realized he was only jesting.

"With that being the prize, how could I choose Dad's? He's already married, so I couldn't choose his even if it was the best. I couldn't help but call it a draw."

She couldn't help laughing along with him as he planted a

kiss on the end of her nose.

"I love you, Kari Lynn."

Their walk took them down the path through the trees and eventually to the old maple tree.

"There's the tree house. Let's go up. I used to love to come out here when the moon was full like tonight. At just the right time it shines in one of the windows and casts its light across the floor. I would come up here and dream all kinds of things I hoped for in the future while I looked at it."

Troy helped her up the ladder and they settled in the old, brown tweed chair in the corner. As they looked out the window at the bright yellow globe in the sky, she couldn't help recalling her dreams for the future.

"I used to think the old man in the moon would grant my every wish. I think I even halfway believed he had some kind of magic he bestowed on people as he sent his spell across the beam that came in the window."

Troy stirred beside her and took her hand in both of his.

"I see what you mean. It does feel magical here with you."

Before long she was pulled into the circle of his arms and held close. She felt the beating of his heart against her breast. If only she could stay right here in his arms. Forever.

"I love you, Kari Lynn, more than you can imagine. You mean more to me than anything in the world."

The rush of tears flooding her eyes made his face appear blurry when she looked at him.

"I love you too. I used to sit here in the moonlight and dream about having someone to love. But I never thought it could be this wonderful to love someone the way I do you. I wish tonight could go on forever."

"It would if you consented to be my wife."

She closed her eyes and shook her head.

"You don't know how easy it would be for me to say yes," she whispered as she buried her face in his shoulder.

"Then say what your heart prompts you to say," he murmured in her ear. "Say you will be my wife."

"I…I can't," she choked out between sobs. "It…it wouldn't be fair to you."

She lifted her face to look into his eyes. Tears streamed down her face, but she didn't try to stop them.

"I just can't convince myself you would be happy without children. And I could never be content knowing how I disappointed you."

Burying her face back in his shoulder again, she reveled in the feel of his arms around her as he rocked her back and forth.

"Shh. Don't cry." His voice was a quiet whisper. "I told you how I felt about this before. You're the one I love, the one I want to spend the rest of my life with."

He cradled her head on his shoulder. Neither spoke.

Thoughts ran wild in Kari Lynn's head. She wanted more than anything in her life to marry him, yet the thought of that one thing she was positive would come between them continued to haunt her.

She tried to think about the possibility of adopting children. Maybe she could come to love a child she didn't give birth to. She served in the nursery at church on occasion, and she always enjoyed holding the babies close, rocking them and singing lullabies until they fell asleep. She did feel a sort of love toward them. Yet it wasn't the same kind she knew she would have for her own child, her own flesh and blood. It simply wouldn't be the same.

An argument raged in her mind. Maybe he would be content without children. Other couples seemed happy without them. Perhaps they could be too.

But as much as she tried to tell herself it would work, she knew it never would. Back and forth the arguments ran through her mind. One moment she considered the idea of adoption, the next moment she shuddered at the thought.

Oh, God, show me what You have for us in the future. Make Your answer so plain I can't help but know what You desire for my life.

A verse of Scripture popped into her mind. "But Jesus said, 'Let the little children come to me and do not hinder them, for to such belongs the kingdom of heaven.'"

She had no idea where that thought came from, although she did recall reading the verse in the book of Matthew during her quiet time the other day. But she didn't know why this particular passage came to mind right now.

Then a startling thought came to her. Maybe this was her answer. Perhaps the Lord was telling her that all the little ones belonged to Him. Even those cast aside by the women giving them birth. If He loved them all, then shouldn't she? But she could never do it without His help.

"Lord," she prayed, "if You want me to love an adopted child then You will have to put that love in my heart. There is no way I can do it on my own. If You want me to marry Troy and have a family, then show me in a way I won't be able to miss."

A peace she had not experienced for some time flowed over her. She knew God had spoken to her heart in His inaudible way, the way He so often did.

After reciting the verse in her mind again, she knew she had no choice. The verse wasn't referring to adoption, she knew that, and she was not one to take a verse out of context and make it say something it wasn't meant to say. Yet God seemed to be telling her that He would give her the love she needed to love even an adopted child. Yes, if He brought one of these little children across her path she would have no choice but to love it. To love it as her own.

Yes, that was her answer. She knew it as clearly as if God spoke to her in an audible voice. He would help her love an adopted child. She could marry Troy. And they would have a family.

She lifted her face and smiled through the tears that continued to run down her face.

"Yes, Troy, I will marry you. I want to be your wife."

She couldn't help the smile that broke through her tears when he sucked in a surprised breath.

"You…you mean it? You will marry me?"

She nodded. "Yes, Troy, I…"

Further words were impossible as his lips covered hers. When he finally pulled away he smiled into her eyes.

"You don't know how long I have waited to hear you say those words."

He kissed her forehead, her eyes, the tip of her nose, then kissed her lips again.

"You're sure you want to marry me?" he asked as though he still couldn't believe he heard right.

She couldn't contain the chuckle that seemed to bubble from her throat at the look on his face.

"Yes, Troy. Nothing could make me happier."

He shook his head and gazed at her for some time.

"What made you change your mind? Not that it makes a difference," he added, "but I am curious. A few minutes ago you seemed certain it wouldn't be fair to me if you married me."

"I just spent a little time talking to God and asked Him to make it plain what He wanted for me in the future. He gave me the fourteenth verse of Matthew nineteen where Jesus said to His disciples, 'Let the little children come to me and do not hinder them, for to such belongs the kingdom of heaven.'"

Troy's brow furrowed and she couldn't help chuckling at the perplexed look on his face.

"How did that speak to you? I don't see what that has to do with our getting married."

"It doesn't. But it does tell me to love the little children God placed on this earth. Those little ones I called castaways, the ones their mothers don't want. They're His children too. Oh, I know that's not what this verse is talking about at all, but it made me realize that God loves these little ones as much as any others. If He sees fit to bring some of these precious ones into our home He will give me the grace to love them. To love them as my own. We'll have children, Troy. We'll have little treasures to bless our home."

His face shone when he smiled at her and pulled her into his arms again.

"I know we're going to be happy, very happy. Thank you, Kari Lynn."

They sat in the moonlight for some time and let the mood of the moment shower around them.

All of a sudden she was nearly dumped out of the chair when Troy jumped to his feet.

"We need to tell your parents. I haven't even asked your dad if I can marry you. As long as they're here we might as well do it right."

He helped her down the ladder's steep steps and they ran hand in hand down the path toward the cabin.

Mr. Moore looked up from the book he was reading when the two excited people burst into the living area.

"You look excited. Anything you care to share?"

Kari Lynn nearly melted when Troy smiled at her before turning to her father.

"Mr. Moore, I would like to ask permission to have your daughter's hand in marriage."

The older man grinned at his wife and then looked at Troy, a serious expression on his face. "Has she consented to marry you?"

"Yes."

"Yes, Daddy, I do want to marry him. More than anything."

Mr. Moore looked from his daughter to Troy.

"Then you have my permission to marry my daughter. May God bless you both."

The room exploded in a mixture of tears, laughter, hugs, and well wishes. It was almost midnight before everyone calmed down enough to go to bed.

As Kari Lynn crawled into bed that night, she didn't think she would ever be able to go to sleep. Snuggled between the blankets, she raised her heart in thanksgiving to God.

"Thank You, Lord," she whispered. "Thank You for making Your will so plain to me by giving me the verse that showed me You will help me love any little ones You bring our way. I know it will only be with Your help I'll be able to do it. Bless our lives together. May our home be filled with Your love and Your joy. And with all the little ones You bring us."

chapter 19

The next November.

Kari Lynn almost jumped out of her chair when her phone rang. The bridal magazine in her hand flew in the air and landed across the room.

"Anne had her baby this morning!" she heard Chad say.

Her hand went to her mouth, the stack of magazines in her lap falling to the floor when she jumped to her feet.

"The baby can't be here. Anne isn't due for another two weeks."

"That's true, but the baby is here. A beautiful little girl, six pounds one ounce, nineteen inches long."

"What happened? Is…is the baby all right? Is Anne okay?"

"Calm down. Everyone is fine. The baby did take us by surprise, but she's perfect in every way." He chuckled as he added, "I guess she knew her mother is to be your maid of honor next month and thought it was time to come."

"You're sure everyone is okay." She still couldn't believe she heard the man right.

"Both baby and mother are doing great. Anne can't wait for you to come and see the little one."

"Can she have visitors?"

"Yes. But if everything goes well she'll go home in the morning. She's anxious to see you."

"I'll see if I can slip up for a few minutes this afternoon. Will that be okay?"

"I'll tell Anne. She looks forward to showing off our little one."

She shook her head and put the phone down, still unable to believe her friend had her baby already.

Tears came to her eyes but she brushed them aside. The emotional wounds from her abortion had pretty much healed, but the thought of her friend with a baby brought back unpleasant memories. She was happy for Chad and Anne, but she still wished she could give birth to a baby of her own some day.

When she walked into Anne's room that afternoon she couldn't help noticing the radiant glow on the new mother's face. A stab of resentment and jealousy threatened to overwhelm her, but she tried to shove the emotions away. She wouldn't spoil this joyous time for the new parents.

Anne held the newborn in her arms and motioned for Kari Lynn to come see her.

She touched the soft hair on the baby's head and sniffed back tears threatening to spill down her face. "She's beautiful." Then looking up at Anne, she asked, "Have you decided on a name?"

"We're still not completely certain, but we think we're going to name her Nicole Page."

"I like that name. She looks like a Nicole."

"Want to hold her?"

She didn't know what she wanted. Although she longed to hold the baby, she was afraid of how she would react. It would be terrible if she burst into tears in front of the happy parents, and it wouldn't take much for them to start rolling down her face. Yet she did yearn to hold the little one.

"May I?"

Trembling arms reached for the infant the mother held toward her. A tear slipped down her cheek as she cuddled the sleeping baby in her arms and she quickly buried her face in the pink blanket, hoping no one noticed. If only she could have a baby of her own someday. But she couldn't let these thoughts ruin the happiness in the room. Lifting her head, she pasted what she hoped was a happy smile on her face.

A minute later the tiny face puckered and an unhappy cry soon followed. Had the little girl read her thoughts and she wanted her mother back?

"What did I do?"

Anne laughed as she held out her arms to take the squalling child.

"Not a thing. It's just mealtime for this little one. I found out in a hurry she is not patient when she thinks it's time to eat."

"I suppose I should leave then."

"You don't have to go. This won't take us long."

"I should be on my way. Things are waiting for me at home." She grinned as she added, "I am planning a wedding, you know. And I'm sure you're tired. I'll visit you again after you get home."

A multitude of emotions flitted across her mind as she drove away from the hospital. She was happy for her friends and knew they were excited about the baby. But when she held the little bundle in her arms for those few minutes it was just another reminder that she would never experience those happy moments for herself. Perhaps someday she would hold a little one in her arms now that she allowed herself to consider adoption, but she still wished she could give birth to her own baby.

Blowing out a frustrated sigh, she forced her attention back to the street and traffic in front of her. No, the joy of bringing a little one of her own into the world would never be hers.

Five days before Christmas

"Are you sure everything is taken care of?" Mrs. Moore asked as she put the last of the dinner dishes in the dishwasher.

Kari Lynn picked up a list from the counter and dropped into a nearby chair. "I hope so. I've gone over this list so many times the last few weeks it's about worn out."

Her dad's arm went around her shoulders.

"Now stop your worrying. Everything will be just fine. If some little thing is overlooked no one will even notice." He grinned at his wife. "Remember our wedding when I almost forgot the rings?" He chuckled. "I did remember them just as I walked out the door, so all went well."

Her hand flew to her mouth.

"I better call Troy and make sure he has ours. It would be terrible if he forgot them."

A call assured her they were tucked safely in the pocket of Chad's tuxedo. He saw to the task himself so knew they would be there when the time came.

"Why don't you lie down and relax for a while and then go to bed early," her mother suggested. "You have run around like a whirlwind ever since we arrived last week. You will be completely worn out by the time you meet Troy at the altar."

"Oh, Mom, there's no way I can relax. Everything will continue to run through my mind as fast as it is now."

She couldn't help picking up the list again and running her finger down the items. "I'm sure I forgot something."

Her mother took the list from her hand and gave her a gentle push toward her bedroom.

"Go run a tub of hot water, put in some bubble bath, and soak for a while to let yourself relax. Then at least rest, even if you don't sleep." She nodded toward her daughter-in-law. "Pam and I can take care of things. And Anne will be here in the morning so she can help us make sure everything is done." Mrs. Moore smiled. "It isn't that long since she was married, so I'm sure she can help us figure out if anything was overlooked."

"I'll try, but I'm not going to promise I won't jump up a million times when I think of something."

As soon as she sank up to her chin in a tub of hot, fragrant bubbles, her taut muscles started to relax. It wasn't long before she felt herself doze off in spite of herself.

Her head was about to slip below the water when she woke with a start. How could she have fallen asleep in the bathtub? Crawling out, she quickly dried off, slipped into a pair of pajamas, and climbed into bed. She knew she wouldn't sleep, especially now since her nap in the tub, but she would humor her mother and at least lie down.

Someone was shaking her shoulder and she woke her with a start. A familiar chuckle brought her awake. "Time to get up if you don't want to leave Troy alone at the church."

She forced her eyes open and stared at the person standing beside her bed. Suddenly it registered what was going on. Throwing back the covers she jumped to her feet.

"Oh, my! What time is it?"

"Don't worry." Anne put out a hand to steady her as she lost her balance. "You have plenty of time. It's just nine o'clock. We have all day."

"Nine in the morning or evening?"

"Morning, silly."

Her head fell into her hands as she dropped back on the edge of the bed.

"I can't believe I slept all night. That hot bubble bath must have really relaxed me." She looked up at Anne. "How long did I sleep, anyway?"

"Your mom said you went to bed about ten last evening."

Although still not fully awake, she jumped up from the bed. Rubbing her eyes she tried to gather her thoughts.

"I better get myself in gear. After all, this is my wedding day."

Shooting another glance at the clock to make sure she did have plenty of time, she grabbed her robe and dashed toward the bathroom.

"I'm glad we figured out what to do with my hair so I don't have to spend half the day deciding what to do with it." She stuck her head around the bathroom door as she added, "Time I don't have."

The remainder of the day was spent getting ready for the wedding. Both Anne and Pam tried to convince her to get some rest so she would be fresh and relaxed when she met her groom. But she insisted she'd had enough sleep last night and refused their advice. The three of them giggled like a bunch of school girls as they decided which color nail polish looked best and what hair style to wear. Several were tried and rejected until all were satisfied.

By four thirty everyone was on the way to the church to get dressed. It was still almost impossible to believe she was getting married.

Just before leaving the dressing room, she paused to take one last look at her reflection in the full length mirror. She hardly recognized the woman looking back at her.

The capped sleeved, floor length dress of white satin overlaid with a filmy layer of organza, flowed behind her in a short chapel train. A modest scooped neckline topped her fitted bodice, accentuating her slim waist. Long blond hair was swept up on the sides with the back left to hang in loose curls around her shoulders. A film of shimmering organza attached to a seed pearl crown hung just below her elbows, covering the tops of her long, fingerless gloves.

Her knees wouldn't stop shaking as she stood outside the sanctuary. In spite of the fact she didn't want Troy to see her until the last minute, she couldn't resist peeking around the door. She smiled as her niece, Stephanie, walked sedately down the white runner to the front of the church. The girl wore an emerald green, floor length dress with a fur headpiece on her long, blond hair. Jordan, looking proud and very grown up, stood next to his uncle Troy. Dressed in a miniature tux he held a white satin pillow with two rings attached with white ribbon bows. A huge smile covered his face and his eyes were fastened on the little girl coming down the aisle scattering rose petals from the basket on her arm.

"Cute, aren't they?" her dad asked. "And I believe Steph is eyeing Jordan the same as he's looking at her."

"They certainly are darling." She couldn't keep from chuckling. "It does look like a budding romance between the two of them, doesn't it? I'm glad I asked them to be part of the wedding party. Did you ever see anyone more proud?"

She pulled in a deep breath as Pam and then Anne followed

Stephanie down the aisle. Both were attired in puff sleeved, floor length, Christmas red dresses. They carried white fur muffs decorated with sprigs of holly and wore matching fur head pieces. It would be her turn next, and she didn't know if her weak knees were going to carry her.

Then she saw Troy. She had to grab her dad's arm to keep from collapsing when she saw him. He was standing straight and tall, so handsome in his black tuxedo. His expression was somewhat hesitant, yet expectant. She couldn't help wondering what he was thinking. Certainly he wasn't as nervous as she was.

As soon as the attendants reached the front of the church Mr. Moore turned to his daughter. "You're next. Ready?" He smiled as he tucked her hand in the crook of his arm. "Nervous?"

She sent him a tremulous smile. In spite of her attempt to remain calm she noticed the Queen's Anne lace surrounding the white orchids in her bouquet quivered.

"I don't know why, but I am. I know this is what God wants for us, but I still can't help being nervous."

The strains of the wedding march began to crescendo. It was their turn to start down the aisle. The moment she stepped through the door Troy must have seen her. A radiant smile lit up his face, replacing his prior sober expression.

Somehow she managed to make it all the way down the aisle. She could hardly wait until her dad handed her over to Troy.

"Take good care of my little girl, son," Mr. Moore whispered as he placed her hand on Troy's arm.

She noticed Troy's gaze never left her face.

"You can count on it, sir."

Kari Lynn didn't know if her legs were going to hold her up. She never dreamed she would be so nervous. After all, this is the day she had waited for so long. The day she would become

Troy's wife. The day she once thought she would never see.

Everything around her seemed to fade until she was hardly aware of what was going on around her. Everything except her and Troy standing hand in hand, ready to pledge themselves to a lifetime together.

When the time came, she hoped she was saying the right words at the right time. The only thing she knew was that she was getting married. It was her dream come true.

It seemed forever until the pastor finally announced, "I now pronounce you husband and wife. Troy, you may kiss your bride."

It was over. She was married. To Troy. The man of her dreams.

She thought certainly her knees would buckle beneath her when she turned and looked into Troy's smiling face.

"I love you, Mrs. Hoffman," he whispered as he pulled her into his arms. She closed her eyes as he placed a gentle kiss on her lips. "You don't know how happy you've made me today."

Then he kissed her again, a little longer this time.

Pastor Sorenson smiled at the happy couple and then turned them to face the crowd of people witnessing their exchange of vows. With a hand on each of their shoulders, he announced to those assembled, "I present to you, Mr. and Mrs. Troy Hoffman."

The recessional began. Troy took his wife's hand in his and led her back up the aisle.

chapter 20

One year later.

Kari Lynn couldn't believe she was a mother. She had wasted so much time hating and blaming God and Troy for ruining her life and bemoaning the fact she would never have a family of her own. But now two beautiful babies were waiting at the hospital for her and Troy to bring home. There was no way she could ever thank God enough for giving her the love she needed to accept an adopted child. She knew if she had continued to refuse to allow herself to adopt, she would have missed some of His greatest blessings.

They never imagined they would be parents this soon when they began checking with adoption agencies six months ago. She was convinced it was only by God's hand they were able to adopt a baby this soon. And not only one, but they were the parents of twins!

Her parents, anxious to see their new grandchildren, were flying to Minneapolis to spend time with Kari Lynn and their new grandbabies. She was on her way to the airport now to meet them, but decided to stop at the hospital on the way. Hopefully the twins were ready to be released today. They were born five days ago, and she was anxious to spend more than a few minutes a day with them.

"Good morning, Mrs. Hoffman," one of the nurses at the desk greeted her as she stepped off the elevator. "You ready to take those babies home?"

Before she could reply, a voice called to her from the direction of the nursery.

"Are you the lady adopting my babies?"

She looked up to see a tall, auburn haired, girl coming toward her. A nod was all Kari Lynn could muster, and she wondered what the teenager wanted.

"Could I talk to you for a minute?"

Afraid her legs were going to give way under her, she grabbed the edge of the desk for support.

"Yes, I…I suppose you can." Her heart pounding overtime in her chest, she motioned to a lounge across from the elevator. "Let's sit over there."

The girl dropped into one of the chairs. The expression on her face gave no clue of what she was about to say. All Kari Lynn could do was collapse on the edge of another chair.

Oh, Lord, don't let her say she isn't going to give them up after all.

"When my babies were born and I first held them in my arms," the girl began, "I started to have second thoughts about giving them up."

Oh God, please don't make me have to give them up now!

She was certain her heart was going to stop. Fumbling with the strap of the purse in her lap, she hardly let herself breath.

Tears came to the girl's eyes and began to roll down her face.

"I know the state of Minnesota says I have ten days after I sign the papers to change my mind about keeping them. But the more I see of them, the more I'm reminded of that awful night nine months ago.

"I was on my way home from a football game at school and took my usual short cut through the trees behind my parent's house." She tossed her long hair over her shoulders and pointed to a long scar above her right eye. "A man attacked me and I was raped and beaten."

With her face buried in her hands her words were muffled as she continued.

"I wish I could love these twins, but every time I look at them I'm reminded all over of that horrible man. I know my resentment and hatred toward him would eventually rub off on my babies and I couldn't bear for that to happen. I'm glad I found someone who will love them the way I would a child conceived in love, not brutality the way these were. I know I would never be a fit mother for them."

When she raised her head, Kari Lynn's heart broke when she saw the agony written on the girl's face. Instead of the sparkle of youth, the brown eyes bore the look of someone much older, someone who had seen horrors a person of her age should never know.

"I'm so sorry," she whispered. "Please know I will love them enough for both of us." She brushed at her own tears with the back of her hand. "Thank you so much for the gift of these children you are giving to my husband and me."

After hesitating a minute she asked, "Do you mind if I pray for you?"

The teenager nodded.

"I think I'd like that."

They bowed their heads.

"Father, please shower Your comfort on this girl. Heal her wounds, both physical and emotional. And thank You for the gift she has given to Troy and me. I'm so glad she didn't take what might have seemed the easy way out and have an abortion." She sniffed back tears as she remembered her own. "May these precious babies come to know Your love as Troy and I raise them to honor and love You."

"Thank you," the teenager said.

She looked at some envelopes in her hand for a moment.

"I didn't know you would be here today, so I planned to leave these at the desk. But I'm glad I have a chance to tell you in person why I decided to give up the babies."

Holding out two of the envelopes she explained, "I wrote them each a letter telling them why I couldn't raise them myself. I would appreciate it if you would give them to the children when they are old enough to understand. I would like them to know some day it wasn't because I didn't love them."

Then she handed another envelope to Kari Lynn.

"This one is for you and your husband. It's a letter telling you what I already explained. There is also a notarized page letting you know I will never change my mind about keeping the babies. They are now legally yours and no one can ever take them away."

Kari Lynn thought her heart was going to break when she saw the anguish on the girl's face as she rose and tuned to leave. All she could do was bow her head and silently ask God to shower His love on this poor, wounded, young woman.

Kari Lynn shifted from one foot to the other. She looked up at Troy and then back at the babies she would take home as soon as someone brought them from the nursery. The nurses seemed to ignore the anxious parents on the other side of the glass. At least that's the way it seemed to the new mother. Her hands trembled, although she tried hard to conceal the fact.

Troy put an arm around her shoulders and pulled her close. "Nervous?"

"Why don't they hurry? I want to get our little babies home."

She smiled at the man beside her.

"Just think, Troy, we're parents. We have twins! I can't believe it."

She looked into her husband's face. "I'm so nervous. I'm so afraid I'll do something wrong. Once we found out we were going to adopt these babies, I read all the books I could find. But I still don't feel prepared. This girl entrusted her precious little ones to our care. What if I don't meet her expectations? Maybe we should have waited a little longer. We've only been married a year."

Troy turned her to face him. A broad smile covered his face.

"Don't worry, honey. You will be a wonderful mother. Remember, these are our children, our very own Melissa Ann and Ryan Scott. No one holds us responsible for how we raise them. No one except God."

Tilting her face toward his, he added, "They are our little bundles of joy, Kari Lynn. Our very own babies. Remember that."

"But they're so tiny. I don't know if I can handle babies that weigh only five pounds."

"You'll do fine. Just because they are a little smaller than some doesn't mean they are any more fragile."

She threw her husband a wary glance. "As if you're an expert in this department."

He just smiled.

A nurse came through the door with a tiny bundle in each arm.

"Mr. and Mrs. Hoffman, are you ready to take your babies home?"

Kari Lynn gave Troy an apprehensive glance. "I think so."

He winked and sent her an encouraging smile.

"You brought clothes for them, didn't you?"

The new mother held up the diaper bag she carried as the nurse started down the hall, motioning for them to follow.

Both bundles were laid on the bed and the nurse stepped back.

The moment Kari Lynn unfolded the pink blanket and touched a tiny hand, little fingers curled around her own. The feel of her daughter's touch brought tears to her eyes.

"I can't believe it, Troy," she whispered. "She's really ours. Our very own baby girl."

Taking the baby in her arms, she held her to her breast. She couldn't stop the tears of joy cascading down her face.

"She's the most beautiful little girl in the world. Our very own precious little gift from God."

Troy put one arm around his wife. His other hand caressed the soft dark hair. He leaned down and placed a gentle kiss on the top of the baby's head. "Welcome to the Hoffman family, Melissa Ann."

The nurse cleared her throat. "Do you want me to dress the other baby?"

"I'm sorry, I suppose we better get them dressed so you can get back to your work. We'll have plenty of time to admire our children when we get them home."

She couldn't keep her hands from trembling as she started to dress the baby in the frilly pink dress and booties she picked out for this special occasion. It was more difficult to dress the little girl than she expected, and she struggled to get a tiny arm into the sleeve.

Out of the corner of her eye she watched Troy remove the blue blankets from around the other baby and begin to dress the little boy. He didn't seem a bit nervous. She could see he was going to be a big help when they got them home.

The nurses strapped the baby carriers in the back seat of the car. Kari Lynn's arms ached to hold one of her little ones, but she knew hospital rules mandated a child be safely secured. They would be home soon. Then she could hold her children all she wanted.

The proud parents stood beside the bassinettes watching as their twins slept. Finally Kari Lynn tore her attention from her babies and turned to face her husband.

"I want to thank you for everything you've done for me, Troy. Thank you for all your help while I was attempting to get my messed up life straightened out. And now you have shown me what a wonderful thing it is to bring these precious little children into our family. Not as outsiders, but as a part of our family and our lives. I love you, Troy Hoffman, and I love our little Melissa and Ryan, our very own babies."

"Any regrets about adopting?"

The new mother looked back at the sleeping babies. She watched the blankets rise and fall with their breathing for a minute. Then she brushed a happy tear from her eye and turned back to her husband.

"None," she whispered. "No regrets at all. I couldn't love them more if I carried them in my own body."

Thoughts ran through her mind as she watched the babies sleep for several minutes. She turned back to Troy and grasped both his hands in her own.

"There's something I need to tell you."

She paused for a moment.

"After the abortion and all the things that happened afterward, I thought all my dreams for the future were shattered. Broken into a million pieces."

She looked up into his face.

"But God has put those scattered pieces I thought were broken for good, back together again."

She smiled into her husband's eyes and squeezed his hands.

"First He gave me a wonderful husband. And now He has given me two beautiful children. The only piece He hasn't put back in place is the part of my dream for my perfect family. I always dreamed two boys and two girls would make the ideal family. Do you suppose that part might also come true?"

Troy's lips brushed across hers.

"I'm glad your dreams have come true, honey. God is so good to us, even after all the grief we gave Him."

He kissed her again.

"I suppose we just have to wait and see what He'll do next."

"Do you think He might bring more little ones our way?"

"Who knows? He is the restorer of shattered dreams. We'll just have to wait and see."

letter from the author

Dear Readers,

Kari Lynn's Shattered Dreams is a fictional story, but the National Memorial for the Unborn is fact. Located in Chattanooga, Tennessee, it is housed in a building which was once the city's only abortion clinic. Through a miracle of God, pro-life Christians in the Chattanooga area purchased the building. Now it's a place where mothers, fathers, and others can come to receive healing from the loss they sustained. The building, which over a span of eighteen years saw the destruction of over 35,000 babies, is now a place of life and hope.

People have come from all over the country to visit the memorial. Many have purchased small brass plaques to place on the fifty-foot granite Wall of Names as a remembrance to the child who was denied the chance to experience life. These plates can include the name of an unborn child, a date, Scripture reference, and/or a message to the child lost by abortion.

If you are thinking about abortion, consider this. It is not a simple process. It isn't just a quick procedure and that's the end of it. Unfortunately, it is something that will affect the rest of your life. You may feel initial relief that you are no longer burdened, for whatever reason, with a child you didn't want. However, the guilt will continue to follow you as long as you live. Even though you attempt to shove it out of your mind it will remain there, condemning you every time you think about it. And you will think about it, more often than you want. When a friend shows you her new baby your guilt will attack you again. You watch children skip down the sidewalk and you wish one of them was your child.

If you are considering an abortion, please take time to think about all the consequences. Not only will you harbor guilt, but there will come a day when you want a child of your own. Statistics have shown that women who had an abortion are more likely either to be unable to conceive or will miscarry if they do become pregnant.

In the story *Kari Lynn's Shattered Dreams*, she noticed an area alongside the memorial. This is the Memory Garden, an area dedicated to the memory of children lost to miscarriage or the stillborn. Brick pavers can be purchased to place there to remember these children.

The grief experienced by those involved with an abortion is often a silent grief, a "secret" carried in silence, one which often increases with time. The Memorial for the Unborn offers a place where those grieving from an abortion can find healing, a place of closure. It's a place to honor the unborn in a tangible way.

If you had an abortion sometime in the past you may be silently suffering over what you did. You may be ashamed to talk to anyone about it because you know what they will think of you. Take heart, all is not lost. There is help for you. The memorial can refer you to a Bible Study support group in your area. For information about the memorial, write to: National Memorial for the Unborn, 6230 Vance Road, Chattanooga, TN 37421. Or call (800) 505-5565. Information is also available on-line at: www.memorialfortheunborn.org.

discussion questions

I hope you enjoyed reading *Kari Lynn's Shattered Dreams* as much as I enjoyed writing it. Please feel free to use the book for your book club or discussion group.

Below are several questions you may wish use to stimulate your discussion.

1. What does God say about abortion? Discuss verses.
2. What does He say about sex before marriage?
3. Was Troy entirely to blame for what happened to Kari Lynn? Was it right for him to shoulder the blame for what happened?
4. Laura encouraged Kari Lynn to talk about what she did, to "get it out in the open." Is it good for us to share our burdens with others? Why or why not?
5. Is forgiveness easy? Why or why not.
6. Is it necessary to forgive ourselves for the things we've done? What does that involve?
7. How do we get back in a right relationship with God if we feel the way Kari Lynn did?
8. Kari Lynn felt what she did to the little baby she carried such a short time was too terrible for God to for-

give. Is there any sin God will not forgive?

9. Kari Lynn thought God turned His back on her because He wasn't answering her pleas. Does He abandon us when we sin? Discuss Matthew 6:14 &15

10. The woman at the table at work said there would be nothing wrong with having an abortion; it wasn't even a baby yet. When does a baby become a baby?

11. Have you heard someone say they believed that in the first months of development a baby is only "a mass of cells"? How do you feel about this statement?

12. Kari Lynn felt adopted children were "castaways," babies thrown away by their birth mother. Was she right?

13. Troy and Kari Lynn visited the National Memorial for the Unborn. Can going to a place like that help in the grieving process?

14. Mrs. Moore told Kari Lynn according to God there are no big or little sins. Was she right or wrong? Can you cite Scripture verses to prove your answer?

DELAINE SWARDSTROM

Delaine Swardstrom is a registered nurse who spent most of her career working in the correctional system. She and her husband, Jack, spent the first two years of their retirement in Germany as missionaries. *Kari Lynn's Shattered Dreams* is Delaine's second novel. Her first, *The Photograph* was published in 2009. Delaine and her husband of more than fifty years live in South Dakota. They have two grown children, five grandchildren, and one great-granddaughter. When she's not writing, Delaine enjoys knitting, crocheting, and reading.

www.BooksbyDelaine.com
www.Facebook.com/BooksbyDelaine